PROMISE

Single Dads, book 3

RJ SCOTT

Love Lane Books

Copyright

Dedication

For Jack, our beloved black Labrador, who at just over fourteen years old, crossed the Rainbow Bridge in September this year. He was the best "good boy" a family could ever have and losing him leaves a huge hole in our house, and in our hearts.

He was our daughter's dog as she grew up, a friend through her worries and fears, and the photo of him with Briony outside the garage door is the best photo of all. He understood autism in a way that amazed us, and was unflinchingly patient with Matt. Losing a pet as loved as Jack is never a good thing, but he taught us patience, and love. He was so very soft to stroke, he had velvety ears and I loved touching them whenever he put his head on my lap.

He will forever be immortalized as "Cap" in the Single Dads series and has inspired every single dog I have written in my novels.

Thank you, Jack, for the love and devotion you gave to us. We miss you.

For my editor, cover artist, beta and proofers - my small army of amazing people who help me not look stupid. And always for my family

Promise

RJ SCOTT

ONE

Leo

I wish I could stop thinking about Jason Banks.

I was up here in my meditation spot to settle my mind, but it was Jason's face that was front and center in my thoughts. It didn't even help that getting up here to the top of the hill had been freaking exhausting. It used to be a matter of running for a few minutes, but as I had my leg in plaster, it had taken me a good half-hour just to get this far.

I pulled out a bowl and water for Cap, with another bottle for me, and stretched my heated muscles, wincing in pain, and wishing the cast I had from mid-thigh down was gone and that I wasn't worried about where the *hell* Jason was, or what the *hell* he was doing.

I'd seen something in him, thought he could do better than being one of the bad guys, and all I wanted to do was find him now.

"You're an idiot," I said to myself, Cap sitting next to me and nudging my good leg. He looked up at me in expectation probably thinking that I was talking to him. So I scratched behind his ears and attempted to chill.

From there, I could see the sparkling water of our swimming pool, as well as Gina doing yoga in her back yard. Which reminded me, I needed to get Eric back for the whole tuna-casserole-not-even-on-a-special-day thing, and I filed that away for later. Given he was spending so much time away from home right now, what with fighting some of the worst fires we'd seen since Paradise, it'd be difficult to slot that in. But as soon as he was home safe, I'd manage it. I didn't doubt he'd make it home okay, because positivity helped, and there was no way I was going to fixate on what might happen to him.

I could see the main road that snaked into the canyon where I lived, and my house looked smaller from up here, but the water of the pool was still visible, and it was on that that I focused for a moment, before I clambered down to sit on the tiny blanket I always took with me in my backpack. Then I concentrated on my family and friends, and the worst of it all, the Cali fires that had taken Eric away from us again.

There was no evidence of smoke on the horizon from the fires that raged up in San Bernardino over one hundred miles away, but that didn't mean I couldn't imagine they were there. I sent up a quick prayer for Eric, knowing he was up in the hills fighting that town destroying monster. He'd been gone four days now; I doubted I'd see much of him for a few weeks with everyone on call, and I worried about him daily or hourly, now that I didn't even have work to distract me.

Cap laid next to me, his nose on his paws, panting softly, and this was how things went when we were out for a run, and even though this was more of an awkward crutch-walk, Cap knew the routine completely. Stop, drink, think. And for me, pray.

I murmured words I'd memorized as a kid in my new home that felt familiar on my tongue and eased me into thinking about why I was up here in the first place.

Today, I feared for Eric, but I it wasn't just that. I had too many demons haunting me for Eric's safety to be *all* I prayed about.

For the first time in a long time, I'd had no one to bring the things I'd seen home to. Eric was on duty right now, but he was spending more and more time at Brady's place anyway, particularly since they'd gotten engaged a few weeks back. And as for Sean, he was working long hours, and anyway, he had Ash and Mia in his life. The three of us *did* sometimes meet each other when we needed it most, but in this last month, for one reason or another, there'd been no one, and then I'd broken my leg, and I guess no one would think I needed them right now.

I could tell God about the nightmares I carried inside me; that was how it went, but up until now, I'd kept my anger to myself. This morning I was saving every thought I had for Eric in the fire zone. Keeping the pain in my heart unspoken was an easy thing to do. I trusted that God could see into my soul, but why would he want to look into mine, I don't know. I wasn't anything special, just a broken kid who'd been given a wonderful second chance but who couldn't forget where his life had begun.

And then there was Jason's face in my thoughts again. The ex con who'd saved Eric's life had been released from prison, and vanished from my radar, and I didn't like it one little bit.

"Where did you go?" I asked the sky, but got nothing back at all.

Cap rolled onto his back, dislodging my grip, and panting. The sun was higher now, and the shade from the trees was lessening.

He knew it was time to go and *I* knew it was time to go. So, even though I didn't feel much better mentally than before my prayer, I scrambled to stand, balancing awkwardly on one crutch and my good leg. I collected the bowl, the water bottles, and the blanket, shoving it all into my backpack and then stood quietly for a moment. The vista of La Jolla laid out before me, the love I found in family and friends, I was thankful for all of it, and I sent up one last part to my prayer.

"Please keep my family and friends safe," I added in a whisper. "Amen."

After a short pause, Cap and I headed back down to the house, him darting in and around me, vanishing back up the hill then coming back to me with a stick so big it overbalanced him. I narrowly avoided being knocked down but managed to swap the stick for his beloved Frisbee, and he danced all around me until I threw it, barking with utter joy.

Answering calls from my siblings while still on my morning walk had become a thing, it seemed. Why did they appear to time it like that I didn't know, but I had a suspicion they'd planted a tracker on me somehow, and as soon as I put on Cap's leash and headed for the hills, that was when they called. It was easier to ignore them when I was running the course I'd created, but now I was using crutches and walking I couldn't even use that as an excuse.

"What now?" I answered with affection because I

didn't mind the calls, I just pretended I did; it was a sibling thing.

"That's no way to answer the phone, Turt."

"Fuck you, Pot."

My younger brother sniggered. Changing my name from what it was, Leo, all the way up to Leonardo, and then making a Ninja Turtle reference, and finally just to Turt, had been his way of fitting in when our parents had first brought him home.

Unfortunately, it had stuck, even though I was a grown-up now, and Reid was a cop the same as me, with a wife and two children. Pot was short for Reid-apottamus, Turt was short for Turtle, and that was it. We'd become Turt and Pot, and it was an affectionate thing that I loved. Only I'd never tell him that because he'd use it to a conniving advantage. The four Byrne siblings carried their stupid nicknames with pride—Pot, Turt, Jax-man, and Loner—and using them often left those outside the circle bemused.

"How's the leg? Still broken?" He snorted at his joke.

"It's been two weeks, so yeah, it's still broken, thank you." Broken, courtesy of a perp who had decided climbing a roof was a good way to get away from my idiot of a partner, which necessitated me following the perp onto said roof, and then falling. One mid-high break in my tibia later and I had a cast from mid-thigh down, which itched like a bitch. I was forced to use up all my sick leave, and I wasn't even being allowed back on desk duty. Fuckers.

"Ouch," Reid tried for concern, but even though he was my brother and I knew he cared, there was clearly something else he wanted to talk about.

"Thought I'd let you know I'm going to paint Mama's room."

"Okay, and?"

"She wants it done, and I need to ask her to babysit for a long weekend in the new year."

"She'd babysit anyway."

"I just want to grease the rails and I wanted you to know in case Jax talks to you."

I snorted at that. Mama would see right through his offer to paint the rooms and why would Jax want to talk to me about it. "Wait, I thought we agreed that Jax was the chief painter of Mom's house?"

Reid let out a derisive snort, "He's busy. Doing what, I don't know."

"Probably running his renovations business and making it even more successful than it already is?" I deadpanned.

"Whatever, he's an asshole."

"You're just pissed off because Toronto beat the Clippers last weekend."

Jax and Reid had a healthy sibling rivalry over basketball teams, and I didn't get involved, as I was more of a hockey fan.

"What kind of asshole supports a Canadian team when we have a perfectly good team not far from here we can root for."

"You're forgetting Jax *is* Canadian," I reminded him, for what must've been the hundredth time.

"Whatever, later."

"Later."

As soon as I managed to make it home, cursing my leg, and life in general, I refilled Cap's water bowl, and he lay flat out in the shade near the AC unit. Then I headed up for a shower, which was an awkward mess in itself, what with wrapping everything in plastic and trying to balance while doing it.

Sean had told me not to push it, but I'd be damned if I was sitting around and doing nothing, so after the shower, I wondered what I could do next. Gardening? Christmas shopping… given it was getting closer to the big day? I'd filled my days so far looking for Jason, thinking about what he was doing, wondering how I could help him, contemplating the kiss we'd shared, and the way I'd shoved him away.

Yeah, none of it would leave my brain because I had too much time on my hands.

Coffee on, standing in my cool kitchen, I stared out the window at the front of my house, down past the paved front yard to next door where Sean had moved when he'd married Asher.

I wished I could shake the feelings of discontent gripping me as I leaned on the counter, all alone in this big house. I wished I could go and visit next door. I had this desperate urge to take Mia to the park. That always helped when melancholy loneliness hit me, but I knew Sean, Asher, and Mia wouldn't be back for an hour or two; some meeting in LA for the adoption they were researching, so there went that idea. They would provide such a good home for a child in need, or children, and I'd already done my bit, writing a statement on the kind of men they were, and now I had to back off while they went through the process.

I was a man of action, the one who organized, cajoled, sorted, and sitting on my hands where the potential adoption was concerned was killing me. Not to mention my other friend being up where the fires were only just getting under control.

A hummingbird flittered past the window, and I let out a heartfelt sigh as it hovered by a bush, dashing back and forth every so often, and then darting over to next door. I followed its trajectory, and couldn't help but smile; there was something about the tiny birds that fascinated me and infuriated Cap. He was yet to catch one, and never would, they were too fast, too wily, and he was never going to win the game of tag when he considered hiding behind a small bush was good enough camouflage not to be seen —*idiot dog.*

A flash of color caught my attention, scarlet against the wood of Ash's porch, and I leaned awkwardly over the sink to get a better look. There was movement, someone standing there, and for a second, I thought it was Ash, and I felt lighter. They were home! I could go visit and make my pitifully lonely day infinitely better with a Mia-hug. Even if she did call me Fido, which was Eric's fault, the asshole. The figure moved again, and I couldn't quite see, but I knew enough to see it wasn't my friends, or Mia, or anyone I recognized. Maybe it was a neighbor? Was I ready to face the possibility of a random tuna bake delivery from Gina-the-vampy-cougar just to see another person right now?

Hell yes, this was another human and someone who might want to talk to me.

"Wanna go for another walk?" I asked Cap, who went straight to the door, nosing at the leash which hung there. He'd go for a hundred walks a day if he could've. I clipped it to his collar, then grabbed keys and my crutch and headed outside, straight across my yard and over to Ash and Sean's.

I could see a man there, broad-shouldered, dressed in jeans and a bright red T-shirt, and from this vague sideways view, I could see he was carrying something heavy.

"Can I help you?" I asked, and he turned to face me. I recognized him immediately, the same man I'd spent the time since my accident obsessing over and trying to find— Jason *freaking* Banks.

"Jason?"

He was standing in front of me, a child in his arms. He had a scruffy beard, blood matted from a cut on his lip, his left eye swelling, and his T-shirt ripped. He was motionless, blue eyes wide, staring at me as if I was going to arrest him. Christ, he was a mess, and desperate. I'd seen that look, too many times to ignore it.

"Jason?" I repeated when he didn't answer.

He snapped back to stare at me, his gaze wary. Years of training kicked in, and I was careful not to move closer because I'd seen this kind of wide-eyed fear and bewilderment before. Jason was haggard, holding the girl tight, and poised to run.

"Help us, please."

TWO

Jason
_____

My words tumbled out in a breathless run-on sentence. *Help us, please.* "I need Eric."

"Eric's not here—"

"But, I knocked next door at the address he gave me," I blurted, and then lowered my tone when Daisy whimpered. "No one answered."

Leo held up his hand in a gesture that I guess was meant to calm me. "Yeah, that's my place, I was out, and I get that—"

"And there was no answer, so I came here, because I know he has friends next door—"

"—he doesn't live here anymore," Leo finished.

"Where has he gone?" I moved back just one step, but he moved forward just as far, and I found myself with my back to a large chaparral broom. I wasn't trapped, but panic fluttered in my chest like the hummingbird in the bush. The last person I wanted to see was Leo.

"Are you okay? Can I help?" he asked me.

"No." I leaned left to pivot away and leave, but I

stumbled, and he immediately reached out to steady me, and I shrugged him off.

"I'm calling 911," he announced and reached into his pocket for his phone, pulling it out and wincing as I lurched forward, off-balance, and knocked it out of his hand.

"No! No cops!"

He stared me down, but I returned his gaze as steadily as I could manage even as he analyzed me. I must have looked like a wild man, with cuts and bruises; I was an ex-con, and I was holding a small child.

"Wanna Daddy," Daisy murmured as if she'd woken from a dream, and that was a random snippet from it. Then, just as quickly, reality must have hit her again, and she began to sob.

"No 911," he stooped to pick up his phone, and this time I made no move to stop him because I had to trust him. I had no one else left. "Why don't you tell me why you don't want me to call 911?" he asked as he pocketed his cell.

"No."

"Is it because of a call to look out for you, Jason? Where have you been? Who is the child? Is someone missing Daisy? Her parents?"

"No. Of course not. I'm... it's me... no."

"Who is Daisy?" he asked, pushing his questions out staccato sharp. "Where's her mom?"

Grief gripped me, and for a moment, I closed my eyes. "I'm her dad," I insisted. "She's my daughter. Her mom is..." I pressed a kiss to Daisy's head and lowered my voice, "she's in the hospital right now, and all I need is someone to..." *help me.*

"Let me call someone," Leo insisted, and there wasn't much I could do if he decided to call this in, but I shifted Daisy in my arms and then shook my head.

"Please. No." I'd done my part in all of this, and now I had Daisy to consider. With her mom in the hospital, I was her only family, and I needed to get her somewhere safe.

Eric had said he'd help, and he was with a man who had kids, he'd told me he owed me, and I wanted him to take Daisy, give her a home until I could sort everything out.

But he wasn't here, and I didn't know what to do next.

"Is she hurt?" Leo asked.

"No, fu—she's okay, tired, I don't know, I'm all…" My words slurred together, and I coughed again, my throat raw. How the hell I was standing, I didn't know. I'd been running for two days, with no sleep, no food, and adrenalin coursing through me.

"She's upset." He looked at Daisy, who was crying quietly against my shoulder, exhausted and overwhelmed by everything. She'd remained awake as long as she could, holding my hand for reassurance, but when we were half an hour from here, she'd lost her fight with sleep. I didn't want her to cry; I wanted her to laugh and live and have everything I couldn't have.

"I know she's crying, but I can't… I don't…"

Leo glanced at me, and I could see the shocked concern in his gaze, then tightened his hold on the Labrador's leash as it tugged toward a hummingbird in the bush. The day was warm, the sky blue, the buzzing of insects and birds filled my head, but time stood still as he stared at me, with obvious wariness and accusation in his expression.

"You're bleeding," he said, "what happened, Jason?"

"Daisy is okay." I couldn't get past the fact that he needed to know that *she* was okay, and then maybe he would stop looking at me as if I was a murderer.

"That's good." He used the tone that cops only use when they're trying to calm someone down. "But *you're* bleeding. Let me put Cap inside, and then I can drive both of you to the emergency room."

I scratched my neck, scarlet on my fingers from a cut that refused to close, the itching had been driving me insane at one point, but now it just bled. I stared at my hand and the blood dispassionately before wiping the red on my jeans. Something was wrong in my head; I couldn't feel pain anymore, just the anxiety flooding me with acid that burned.

"I need Eric," I repeated. Eric would help me; he said he would.

"But you've got me," Leo said.

Great. I wanted a man whose life I'd saved, who said he owed me and would do anything I wanted to help me when I got out. But what did I have instead? A cop who was dangerously close, telling me that he wanted to take me to an emergency room. That couldn't happen.

"I have to go," I blurted and stepped back and away.

"Wait, we can call Eric if that is who you want."

"It's okay. We're fine."

"You asked for help; I can help. Eric is my best friend, and he would want me to help you. Jason?"

I stopped walking and waited for him to continue.

"You can trust me," he said.

Trust was in short supply. I'd trusted Rainbow to look after our daughter and not give in to drugs. I'd trusted the

Feds, and still, Billy had found Daisy and me. I didn't know who I could trust right now, and Billy had said he'd always find me, and unless I gave him money then next time it would be Daisy that he hurt.

So, yeah, I wasn't ready to trust the cop who had kissed me at the same time he told me he shouldn't be kissing me at all. Fuck him and the horse he rode in on.

I wanted to cry like Daisy, exhaustion pushing me over the edge. "I just need Daisy to..." *be able to sleep somewhere, safe, and with a future that meant something with a family who loved her.* I stopped talking again. The painful silence with Leo staring at me made everything a million times worse.

"What do you need for Daisy?" Leo had taken a step toward me.

I tightened my hold on Daisy, who had stopped crying and was now hiccupping against my neck. "I have to go. We're okay."

"Just come in for a few minutes, you can get cleaned up, let me get you Band-Aids, something to drink and eat at least."

The thought of water, or maybe some food, and anything to stop my neck from bleeding, and somewhere safe to sit with Daisy for a moment, sounded wonderful, the noise of it drowning out my instinct not to trust.

I had to believe that even if Eric wasn't here, maybe Leo was right. He was Eric's best friend, had specifically sat next to me in the hospital and held my hand when I was in pain, then thanked me and told me he owed me as much as Eric did. Back then, in the days after the fire, I'd never wanted him to leave, an attraction between us that transcended the fact he was a cop, and I was nothing.

Asking him to stay in the room had been impossible, and sometimes I'd pretended to be asleep just so I wouldn't get carried away with all the possibilities in my head.

At the event where I'd been awarded a medal for bravery when he'd followed me into the bathroom, he told me he'd do anything I needed so I could get out of jail early. We argued so hard, and he was all up in my face telling me he could fix things. For a brief moment, I wanted him to help me, but I had to tell him no. He'd kissed me so I'd stop talking and when he stood back, I saw the disgust on his face. Not at me, no, he came back for another kiss.

And I'd kissed him back.

He'd been upset with himself, lowering himself to my level, kissing one of the bad guys, and I knew I was right when he shook his head. *What am I doing?* He'd said that to the empty room, and left before I could talk anymore.

I hadn't wanted him interfering anyway.

"No hospital." My words slurred with exhaustion and pain, and I had to have that final wall there. A wall he'd promised not to push through. Leo was dangerous to my safety, and to Daisy, and I needed him to tell me he'd do what I asked.

"No hospital," he agreed, and then he supported my weight, and somehow, we made it into what used to be Eric's house.

THREE

Leo

_____

EVERYTHING I WAS as a cop and a human was at war.

No hospital? Why in God's name had I agreed to that?

I was thinking Amber alert, a mugging, a kidnapping, drugs, guns, hell, I was running every possible scenario through my head. I had compassion for a man who'd seemed like he might be one of the good guys after prison and was somehow in my neighborhood, clearly having been beaten up. Was this a custody battle? I'd seen this before, kids used as pawns, or fought over in bloody marital battles, or kidnapped. Kids terrified they'll lose a parent, scared to think they might never see their mom or dad again.

But she's sleeping in his arms.

I saw the way he was holding the girl, Daisy, but there was guilt and a flash of panic in his eyes. Years of pain and fear inside me fought to the surface, and I had to fight my instinct to grab the child and protect her. I needed to connect with him, talk him off the edge, and so far, it was all going to shit. *Forget it's Jason and focus on what you*

know best. Is there an Amber alert out for her? What had
he done? What was he running from? Why did he need
Eric?

Jason had never been far from my thoughts, not just
because of his case, but because, despite my best
intentions, I was attracted to him. When I'd met him in the
hospital, he'd been stoic most of the time, and at the award
event after he'd seemed cautious but calm, with ambition
and confidence in his eyes. It was this intense hope in him
that I'd been attracted to, and the reason I'd taken my
chance and kissed him in the bathroom at the firehouse. It
had been a vow of sorts, that one day I'd find him, and
together we could work through this weird-ass cop/con
thing we had buzzing between us.

That kiss had never left my thoughts, the irony of me
lusting after a convict was something that didn't sit right
with me, but the kiss had been as explosive as it had been
gentle, and I'd wanted him so bad. Hell, I'd broken a
million rules that day, nearly promised him the earth so
he'd smile at me, and then the kiss.

Stupid-ass attraction.

I knew for a fact that Eric would've done anything for
Jason. So I would as well. Jason had saved Eric, at huge
personal risk, and all of us owed him for his heroism. I'd
gotten a good feeling about him, not because of what he'd
done for Eric, but because his focus was clear, and he
appeared to have drive. I'd gone a lot further than shaking
his hand, told him I could help if he needed me, and then,
of course, there had been *that* kiss.

Only a soft kiss, but the taste of him had been
intoxicating, and I'd very much wanted to kiss him again,
despite the fact I was a cop, and he was a con. *I shouldn't*

have done that. The words haunted me to this day, particularly when the soft, almost hopeful expression on Jason's face had vanished and had been replaced by a hardness that scared me.

"Okay," he murmured.

For a moment, I'd forgotten what we were talking about. Me taking him into the house—that was what we'd landed on. But the questions remained. Why was he bleeding? What the hell was going on here? He'd said that, *of course*, no one was missing Daisy, but there wasn't really any "of course" about this situation, and my predisposition to following the law was yelling at me to *do something official.*

He'd saved Eric, versus what I should have been doing.

I wished I hadn't seen the depths that some people had fallen to in their lives, wished I hadn't rescued kids from the most awful of situations, then maybe I wouldn't have had this stone of dread inside my chest.

"I'll get you a drink, call Eric, see what he says, okay?"

And while I'm at it I'll call the station, check out any BOLOs, or Amber alerts, make this official, get Family Services out here.

I opened the door and let him in, Cap reluctantly going with me, at first prancing and then dragging back, pissed that he hadn't gotten the promised walk. "Come inside." I watched him from there, saw the indecision, then he followed me in. How had he even gotten here? Bus maybe? A cab? And was he Daisy's dad? I didn't recall him having kids in the background check I'd run on him, or in the case notes for his criminal case, and I'd dug a long way down, and was actually waiting on the final batch of reports on the company he'd embezzled from.

He hovered just inside the front door, and I caught his gaze; he was so torn, and I didn't know what to say. So I stayed quiet.

He finally came in and closed the door then edged into my kitchen.

"We don't have anywhere else to go," he half-whispered, and wouldn't quite look me in the eye. "I'm sorry to do this, and if it wasn't for Daisy, I wouldn't have come here."

For some reason, his softly spoken words broke my stubborn cop's heart.

"Jason?" He glanced up then, and when I had his attention, I continued. "Tell me about Daisy."

He buried his nose in her blonde hair.

"She needs to be somewhere safe."

Daisy moved restlessly on his shoulder, and I approached with caution until I could reach out and touch her forehead. She didn't seem that hot, not any hotter than a child asleep on a person's shoulder, on a warm November day. I wasn't an expert, but it seemed to me that she wasn't running a fever. Jason held her with so much tenderness, cradling her with love.

I saw the same thing in him then that I had done all those months ago at the awards ceremony; a spark of life inside him, a desperate need to do the right thing. It was the emotions I'd reacted to when I kissed him.

And the reason I couldn't get him out of my mind.

Jason had spent the last three months since getting out of prison avoiding all contact with Eric, who'd tried his hardest to connect with the man who'd saved his life. Not to mention involving me in attempting to track him down. I'd tried, but Jason had disappeared from the radar, even blowing off the mandatory post-release meetings, for which he would have been heading for trouble had anyone done anything about it. Only, his name wasn't on any lists, and I couldn't understand why the cops hadn't been called in to follow up on his release if he'd vanished so thoroughly. He didn't look as good as he had been at the event, not bright and focused with lips that needed kissing. No, he was beaten up and trampled down, and, if anything, he looked worse than when I'd visited Eric in the hospital and gone next door to thank Jason for what he'd done.

Back then, Jason had been swathed in bandages, off his head on painkillers, burned, and coughing up a lung. I'd been so damn thankful that he'd saved my best friend and I'd visited him every day in the hospital. Sometimes he'd been sleeping, and I'd linger for a few moments to watch him from the door, other times we'd talked, but it was never much of a conversation. My stupid heart had connected with him somehow, and I'd offered to help him, as a thank-you for what he'd done.

I still don't know why.

I switched focus to examine the bruises on his neck, along with the cuts. It looked as if he'd been strangled, and everything in me screamed one thing—whatever compassion and pity I'd felt for him, something here was very, *very*, wrong.

FOUR

Jason

I saw the way Leo stared at me, with horror and then clear-eyed laser attention. In jeans and a shirt, he didn't look much like a cop, or any kind of authority figure, his long hair in messy layers, but his green eyes were focused on me now. Leo was in cop mode.

"I've been looking for you," he said.

"Why?"

"I wanted to help you, after we...y'know, in the bathroom, when we—"

"When you kissed me and then told me to fuck off?" Temper flared in me, but it was short lived and I hated that the memory had forced its way into my head. I needed help for Daisy, not a repeat of his hate.

"Why don't you tell me what happened?" His tone was serious but encouraging, and I went on the defensive.

"I can't," I blurted, and he tensed.

He held out his arms, "Why don't you let me take Daisy?"

No. Fuck no. I'm not letting anyone touch her again.

"No."

"Jason, we should look at your injuries, you're bleeding."

I knew I shouldn't have come, but I didn't have any choice. Billy would have no idea that I'd ask Eric for help. At least not yet, not until he put two and two together and considered the possibility I'd go to the man I'd saved for assistance, but I wasn't taking the chance of anyone knowing where I was.

He can't take Daisy; she's my daughter.

The Feds had said it would only be a few weeks, and then maybe Daisy and I could make that fresh start a long way from here, in the town where I thought she had been growing up safely. They'd built a case against Silas, and now they just had one loose end, finding Billy before he found me.

"She's fine," I copied Leo's tone and attempted to pick something out of his micro-expressions. He wasn't reaching for his phone again, he didn't appear armed, and after that single step closer, he'd stayed back. But his green eyes were troubled, and he was clearly torn as if he had a hundred questions in his head, and maybe that cop's instinct was outweighing trust. I couldn't tell him anything, I'd promised to keep my mouth shut, just as I had four years ago, anything so I wouldn't lose Daisy.

I'd never lose her.

Finally, after we'd stared at each other in a face-off, Leo's shoulders dropped a little, and the tension in him eased. He'd decided that he didn't need to fight, that much was certain.

"How about I get you both a drink, okay?"

This was a perfectly normal house, nothing to hurt

Daisy here, with a wide hallway, and I shivered at the wash of cool air from a working AC, and a cold drink sounded good. He crutched into the kitchen, and I knew I should've asked what he'd done to his leg, but all I did was follow him.

"You should sit," he instructed in a tone that I imagined no one argued with. The stools by the counter were high, and I moved toward them, unsure how I would get up on one with Daisy in my arms. My head felt as if it was stuffed with cotton wool, pain at my temples, my vision blurry. I'd hit the ground hard after that last hit, and I knew I'd done something to myself, maybe even a concussion, although my vision was okay, and I wasn't feeling sick.

Something in my shaky hesitation must have made him reconsider. "Actually, why don't you go through to the sofa and make Daisy comfortable for a while. I'll bring the drinks."

I'd seen his phone when he'd pulled it out of his pocket, and had a very real fear that as soon as my back was turned, he would call someone. "We'll go in together." I was defiant and attempted to stand as tall and steady as I could.

He looked confused, but after a short pause, he turned his back to me, preparing coffee and cold drinks, including a sippy cup of no-sugar juice, and a plate of cookies, which he piled onto one plate and balanced precariously in one hand.

I'm so hungry.

I could've eaten the entire plate, but that would have made me sick. Any food I'd been able to get in the last few days had been for Daisy, and we would have been fine, but when we'd woken up in the city on a bus to nowhere, and she cried in my arms with frustration and confusion, I knew that restless and pointless traveling wasn't sustainable. We had no money, and we had to stop, and right here was as good a place as any for today. I knew Eric had a doctor friend, Sean, who could check out my injuries and maybe even bandage the cuts to make them less obvious. We needed help, and I hoped that Eric would feel like he could do the one thing I needed him to do— give me and Daisy somewhere safe to stay. Then, in a few weeks, when the Feds finally found Billy, we could leave and start new lives away from here.

I didn't know where we'd go; it wasn't as if my family would be interested in welcoming the black sheep into the fold. Vermont sounded good, and I was drawn to it only because of a poster in the bus station that spoke of fall on the East Coast. It was the opposite side of the country, where the leaves would be turning right now, and where I could change my name, and make a new life for myself and my daughter. I'd pick up work, I was good with computers, although I was staying away from those after what I'd done. I was good with my hands, good with engines, quick to learn new skills, and I could earn money somehow. Maybe I could get back into music, get Daisy into a good school, make things *better*.

Yeah, and there goes a flying fucking pig.

"This way," Leo murmured, and left the kitchen with the plate, quite quickly for someone with his leg in a cast. The scent of cookies was enough for me to follow, my stomach growling, feeling lightheaded. I couldn't recall the last moment I'd eaten. Friday maybe? What was today? I had no idea. He led us into a large front room, with huge sofas that I could've sunk into and stayed there. The television was enormous, a gaming machine plugged in, and the detritus of normal living scattered all over—a coffee mug on the small table, magazines, a John Grisham novel, and the AC chilling the interior.

I just need time to work it all out, and someone to check on Daisy.

I sat on the sofa nearest the kitchen, perched on the edge, Daisy stirring in my arms. She'd slept on and off for the last two hours, her sleeping patterns disturbed by everything that had happened in the past few days. "You can lay her down if you want," Leo bent over the side of the sofa he was sitting on, coming up with a handful of blankets and a soft toy. "These are Mia's favorites; she's Asher and Sean's daughter. Do you remember them?"

"The doctor," I said, and felt stupidly fucking proud when he gave me a soft smile.

He reached over to hand everything to me, and after only a moment's hesitation, I took them and laid them next to me. My vision blurred as I stared down at Daisy, and I blinked away the sudden need to close my eyes and never open them again.

What if he snatches Daisy when I lay her down?

I pressed a hand to my sore chest and rubbed, watching Leo settle back into the sofa, wincing as he stretched his legs in front of him. His cast meant I'd have time to get to her if he made a move, and he'd taken a coffee with him, and one of the fat cookies filled to bursting with chocolate. Was he trying to reassure me that he was relaxed? That he wasn't poised to snatch Daisy from my arms or shove me away? The pain in my chest had been growing steadily worse. There was blood on my hand from my neck, and the scarring on my arm itched like nothing I'd ever experienced before. I was a wreck.

At least Daisy is okay.

One-handed, I spread out the blankets and made a secure space for her, then laid her down gently, brushing her blonde bangs from her face and watching as she mumbled, then turned onto her side, her thumb in her mouth, her other hand gripping the blanket. She hadn't wanted to sleep as we'd waited for the bus, it was exhaustion that made her close her eyes, but she was trusting me to look after her.

"She'll be fine," Leo sipped his coffee, watching me over the mug. "Drink something; are you hungry?"

I wanted to eat, but I was fixated on one thing only. "You said we could call Eric?"

He regarded me steadily. "I'm going to be honest with you, I doubt we'll reach him, he's working up in the hills. But we can try after you've had a drink and something to eat. Yeah?"

I winced, and even though Leo sat watching me, I wasn't going to be intimidated by his steely gaze. I'd seen him react to kissing me, seen his self-loathing and anger, and I'd promised myself I'd never talk to him again. He'd given me a brief hope then snatched it away in the cruelest of fashion and the last thing I wanted was to be anywhere near him. "I'm not sitting here with you," I snapped. "I need to talk to Eric."

"And as I said, he's in the hills at the San Bernardino fire," Leo said, and I caught fear in his voice at the same time as he was trying for being all calm and in control.

I wish I was up there with Eric, and that Daisy was safe with her mom in Vermont, and that I had a normal freaking life. Part of me had hoped that post-prison I could think of a full-time firefighting career, but a criminal record meant I couldn't do the EMT portion of the training, so that meant no career. But, that didn't mean I wasn't aware of what was happening all over California right now. But I knew the fear, and something twisted inside me, thinking Eric was out there facing the flames. The latest of so many fires had been fast-spreading, and it was only fifty percent contained and had burned nearly fifteen square miles, forcing over ten thousand people to evacuate. Leo kept talking, but all I could hear were random words, and none of them made sense. I shuffled forward on my chair, which was difficult because the softness of it was sucking me back in. I was exhausted, ached, smelled like a ten-day-old roadkill, and my head hurt so bad. Sleep was yanking at me as hard as it was Daisy.

"...so, yeah, I'll call his partner, Brady. Do you remember him from the award ceremony, with Maddie and Lucas?"

"Uh-huh." A normal family, lovely kids, Eric and Brady. I remember.

"I'll see if Brady has any news, but we have a group chat, and the last update was that Eric was bunking up there."

I pulled myself back to the talking part of this whole thing. "Eric said I could call him, and I tried to," I coughed, my throat tight. "I used my burner phone, so he maybe wouldn't have known it was me..." Leo's eyes widened fractionally, and I realized I'd just admitted I had a goddamn burner phone.

"Why do you have a burner phone?" Leo asked. At

least he hadn't jumped up, found his gun, and arrested me on the spot, but he was suspicious, and I should have kept my mouth shut. I ignored the question, almost hoped he would forget he'd even heard what I said, and forged ahead.

"There's no reply from Eric to my messages the last few days, but I get that now, I should have realized he would be on duty…" I wasn't making sense, but if Eric wasn't here, what did that mean for Daisy and me?

"Daisy looks like she needs to sleep for a week," he observed, and I felt immediately guilty.

"We've been traveling."

"Where from?"

Great. Why the hell did he even need to know that?

"North," I said, fully aware that could be everything from a few miles away to right up in Canada.

He wore a neutral expression, didn't seem skeptical or anything like that, then waited for a beat before answering. "I don't recall anything in your file that indicated you had a daughter."

"I told you not to look," I snapped.

"I'm a cop," he said, evenly. "You know I've seen your file, and I've been looking for you since you go out."

"Why?"

"I wanted to see if extenuating circumstances could get you out early. I told you that." I didn't want any attention on me, and I'd told him to keep away. He'd given me this stubborn look, but no one was going to dig into things that I wanted to be left alone. And then, of course, he'd kissed me, and rocked my entire fucking world, promising me he'd help, and then regretting the kiss as soon as he was done.

I wanted to break down and tell someone, *anyone*, what had happened, what I'd done, and what had been done to me. But why did it have to be Leo?

"Daisy *is* my daughter, and I need her to be safe," was all I said because my head was stuffed with a mess I couldn't untangle, so many threads all woven into a knot that hurt so bad. I took one of the cookies, nibbling at the edge, the taste of chocolate overwhelming, and slid down in the chair a little to ease the pain in my back.

"Okay," he said with a shrug. "Finish your cookie, and we can talk about contacting Eric."

I nodded, a wave of dizziness passed over me, and I bit off more cookie. The last thing Daisy needed was her dad fainting, but the pain in my chest was tight, and I was so tired that not even terror could've kept me awake. I tried my hardest to fight, but I lost.

WHEN I WOKE UP, Daisy wasn't next to me, and then I heard her shout.

"Daddy!"

FIVE

Leo

—————

I WAITED until Jason was asleep or unconscious—I couldn't tell, but at least he was breathing in a gentle rhythm. I watched as he fought and scrapped his way to stay awake until abruptly, his eyes shut, and he slumped into the corner, and the exhaustion that marked his face finally stole him away. His hand fell to his side, resting on the little girl who was so much like him, the half-eaten cookie tumbling to the floor which Cap found. Finally, I got a closer look at Jason and checked his pulse; it was thready, but there.

He was still as gorgeous as I'd first thought all those months ago, grubby, exhausted, and verging on too thin, I could still see the cheekbones, and the stubborn tilt to his chin, the longest eyelashes, and the red of his full lips. I'd been attracted to him in the hospital, and at the awards ceremony, but had always put it down to feeling incredibly grateful that he'd put himself between an inferno and Eric. I imagined that seeing him as a hero outweighed the fact he was still a convict, even as the

Mayor put a medal around his neck and handed him a commendation.

"What do you want from Eric?" I murmured, and at the sound of my voice, Daisy stirred. Instinctively, I gathered her into my arms. I didn't know what Jason was doing, holding her and running with her, but I needed to call Sean to come and check her out. I shouldn't have been sitting there staring at a man I had no business even checking out; I should've been considering that there was a child who needed my help. I wished someone had done this for me all those years ago before Mama and Papa Byrne took me in. I went into the kitchen and called Sean immediately.

"Get home now," I demanded before Sean even had a chance to ask me why I was calling.

"What—?"

"It's an emergency."

"Jeez, I'm five minutes away, asshole," Sean muttered good-naturedly, "what's so important?"

I could've explained to Sean what was going on, but what was the point? "It's a medical emergency, get over to the house as soon as you pull up." I ended the call and rocked Daisy in my arms. That was a pretty name for a very sweet little girl. She was clean, her top tidy, her jeans fresh, but a check in the bag Jason had dropped by the sofa revealed other clothes for her, along with a couple of reading books and a stuffed red dragon. However Jason had ended up appearing as fucked up as he did, he'd taken care of Daisy, and she'd been sleeping in his arms, so she trusted him.

One-handed, I pulled out my laptop and ran a few searches on missing children, and briefly checked every dead-end, and any open cases, and there was nothing about

Jason or Daisy. So if she wasn't a kidnapped child, then there must have been another reason why Jason was so scared.

I wanted to log the information with my lieutenant, bare details about Jason and Daisy arriving at my house, but something stopped me, and it was in large part because I'd promised him I wouldn't.

This is so fucked up. I don't mess about with my duty. What the hell is happening to me? Daisy woke up as I was second-guessing myself, and I saw she had the same startlingly blue eyes as Jason. She stared right at me, unfocused and scared, and then let out a disturbing squeal, before wriggling to get away from me. *I'd just wanted to check her out, only wanted to help.*

Well, I fucked up there.

I helped her down, made sure she was standing on her own, and she stared up at me as if I was going to kill her. Why the hell did I think it was a good idea to pick her up? I was a stranger; I wasn't in uniform. I was a fucking stupid idiot.

"I'm a cop, Daisy. It's okay."

Cap was instantly there, standing next to her, waiting for an instruction from either of us. He was familiar with children, loved Mia, but Daisy seemed to be a year or so older than Mia, and I didn't think Daisy was used to dogs, as she shoved him. Of course, in his usual big-bear way, he just veered off and didn't take offense.

"Go away!" she ordered Cap, with imperious force, and he moved back a few paw-steps and sat next to the stool. "I want my daddy."

"Daisy? I'll get your daddy. It's okay. I'm a policeman—"

"Where's my Daddy!" she shouted. "DADDY!"

I bent to talk to her, but she hid even farther behind a stool, her eyes were round and wide, and not even my best soft voice helped. I was this close to holding my hands up when Jason stumbled blindly into the kitchen, calling her name in panic, then yanking at chairs to get to her before scooping her up into his arms.

"Daddy!" she whimpered, and he held her close, tight, and she buried her face in his neck.

"Stay away from her," he ordered, his free hand clenched in front of him, swaying, and his eyes burning with anger. That was the moment I held up my hands to both of them.

"I was just going to get her a drink," I lied.

"Leave us alone."

Okay, this wasn't going well, and Jason was going to keel over at any moment. He took a step toward the door, and then another, and I could imagine him vanishing, and the cop instinct in me overtook the confusion I was feeling. "Stop," I demanded, and he stiffened and turned back to face me, his eyes wide and his grip on Daisy so hard she wriggled against it.

"You can't make us stay."

"It's best for Daisy if you stay." I tried to remain calm, already calculating how to catch him if he attempted to leave. I needed to make sense of the situation, of him with bruises and cuts, and of Daisy.

"You can't fuc— stop us from leaving." He paled again and swayed a little.

"I'm not trying to stop you, but Jason—"

"I'm going."

I moved so fast I nearly threw my back out and face-

planted, getting between him and the door, Cap tangling in
my legs. I bet that all Cap could think was that this was
one fun game, and I needed him not to trip me up right
now. "Steady," I reassured him, and he sat at my side as if
he was ready to play more of this running-real-fast-in-a-
kitchen game.

Jason stumbled back in shock, and I was equally
worried that he'd misstep and fall. This was getting out of
hand way too fast.

I held up my hands. "You can trust me. Look, I'm not
going to hurt you, but I'm worried about your daughter. Do
you remember Sean? He's a doctor, I called him, and he'll
come over and check her out, and then you and I can sit
down, and you can explain what's wrong, and we can try
and get hold of Eric."

He winced, wavered in indecision, but when the door
opened behind me, he went into an immediate half-crouch
in the corner, protecting Daisy with his body. What the
hell?

"Did you cut yourself on some paper again?" Sean
deadpanned. But his smile dropped when he took in the
situation, with Daisy whimpering. Sean reacted fast,
slipped into doctor-mode in an instant, and went to his
knees next to the two of them.

"Jason?" He sounded incredulous, and I backed away
to give him space. "Hey, who is this you have here?"

"Daisy," Jason managed after a short pause, and my
heart broke for him as he held her so protectively.

"Hello, Daisy," Seam murmured. "My name is Doctor
Sean, can you let me help you, sweetheart?" Sean reached
for Daisy, but she went quiet and looked to her dad for
reassurance.

The situation wasn't helped by the fact Jason didn't want to let Daisy go.

"I can help Daisy," Sean told him. "You can let her go," he added, but there was fear and indecision on Jason's face.

"Okay," Jason mumbled and uncurled her hands from the grip she had on him, whispering reassurances to her.

"What happened?" Sean asked me, remaining calm and easing Daisy from Jason's grasp. Jason attempted one last time to keep hold of her, but his eyes rolled in his head, and I swear he was *this* close to passing out again. He slumped back in the corner, defeat in every line of him, his hands outstretched as if he wanted to tug Daisy back. Sean went straight into the kitchen, setting Daisy on the counter and stepping back enough to examine her. He'd prioritized the child who had blood on her shirt. "Hello, sweetheart," he began in a soft voice. She nodded mutely. "Do you hurt anywhere?"

She shook her head, her blonde curls bobbing, and her beautiful blue eyes filled with tears. "Help Daddy."

I bent over next to Jason, who mumbled something, and gripped my arm.

"Your daddy will be okay," I lied to Daisy.

"You have to help him." A mini-Jason was evident in the defiant tilt of her tiny pointed chin. There was a sudden stubborn spark of life in her eyes, a determination to make people believe what she was saying.

Sean pressed a hand to her forehead, and then to her neck, nothing too obvious, but I guessed it was enough to get some kind of initial readings. The front door opened, and Cap danced around Asher, who came in grinning, Sean's medical bag in one hand and Mia in his arms.

"Uncle Fido!" she squealed, and I smiled at that normality.

"What did you do to yourself?" Ash asked me with a grin, which fell from his face when he saw Sean, Jason, and Daisy in the kitchen. Without saying a word, he handed the bag to Sean and backed away. Finished with Daisy, Sean set her on the floor, and she immediately went to Jason's side. Sean followed her and crouched next to Jason, opening his kit and pulling out a stethoscope, doing checks I'd seen a million times.

"What happened?" Ash asked me and grabbed hold of Cap, who wanted to play with Mia.

"I don't know." I had no freaking idea what was happening. If it wasn't for the fact that Jason had saved Eric's life, then I would have put in a goddamned 911 call by now. My first responsibility, whatever Jason had done for Eric, was to keep Daisy safe, check for Amber alerts, get her away from him, *just in case.* But Sean was examining Jason, asking him quiet questions, and he only hesitated when he reached the bruising at Jason's neck.

"Can you tell me about these?" Sean asked Jason, who was half awake and only semi-lucid, and I held my breath while next to me, Asher went still.

"He wouldn't let Daddy go," Daisy said, and her lower lip trembled, tears rolling down her cheeks. I'd seen kids like this before, where crying happened quietly, in case they were heard. What in God's name had this poor kid seen in her life? What part had Jason played in it? He'd been in prison, and she wasn't very old, I couldn't make sense of any of this.

"Who wouldn't let your Daddy go?" Sean asked as he lifted Jason's shirt and examined his belly. Jason pushed him away and clambered to stand, only swaying a little, one hand on the wall.

"Don't you tell them, Daisy," Jason snapped, and that got my back up.

"An' he hurt my momma," Daisy blurted.

"Daisy stop!" Jason said more loudly.

"Don't shout at me!" Daisy cried.

I held up a hand to stop him. "Who hurt your momma, sweetheart?" This was the first real mention of a mom.

"An' me," she added and screwed her eyes tight. Did someone hurt her? Memories of abuse cases muddled and sparked with my childhood memories, a perfect storm of chaos in my head, and I saw red.

"Who, darling?" Sean prompted.

"Daddy-B hurt momma and then me," she slurred with a sob, all I heard was the word daddy and hurt, and that was it, I lost what little control I had. Pushing past the awkwardness of my leg, past a stool, and narrowly avoiding Cap, I moved so quick that Jason didn't see me coming. I forced myself between him and Daisy, pushing Sean aside, shoving Jason back as he yelped in pain until I had him pinned to the door, trying not to cause any more injuries to the man covered in blood and to keep my temper in check. He tried to scramble free, and I turned him, so his belly was against the wall and twisted his left arm behind his back. As far as I was concerned, kiss or no kiss, and whatever the hell I owed him for saving Eric's life, this fucker who hurt kids was under arrest.

"Let me go," he shouted and tried to move. Still, I might have had a broken leg, but he was weak and slow, I had forty pounds on him, and six inches in height, not to mention police training. He was going nowhere.

"Daddy! Daddy!" Daisy was wailing, Jason shoving me back, Sean at my elbow, but the red mist had descended. I should have called this in the first moment I'd seen him on the porch next door.

"Someone call 911!" I snarled, a lifetime of pain and fear front and center as I pushed on his hand. Part of me, the dark hidden places inside my soul, demanded that I hurt Jason, and hurt him bad. I'd seen too much pain like this, too many kids on the streets, or in run-down houses with junkie parents. I was here to protect kids like Daisy, and Jason was not fucking moving unless I let him.

"Let him go, Leo," Ash pleaded, Sean there as well, both talking at me, Cap whimpering and butting my leg, and then Daisy's voice broke through the temper.

"Let my daddy go! Let him go!"

"It wasn't him who hurt her," Sean attempted to pull me away, opening my fingers in their grip, and tugging. Finally, I was off him, and Jason slumped to the floor, Daisy sobbing loudly and throwing herself into Jason's arms.

"What the hell?"

Jason stared up at me. "I wouldn't hurt Daisy. I got Daisy away. It was someone else; he was the one who... Look, we don't have anywhere to go," he said. "Why won't someone just fucking help us?"

"I hate you! Don't hurt my daddy!" Daisy shouted at the room, and it didn't make sense until I realized she was pointing at me. "I hate you," she sobbed and gripped Jason's leg before he lifted her, wincing as he moved, pain carved into his features.

Two things were clear at that moment, Daisy was protecting Jason, and Jason had protected Daisy. They were looking out for each other. There was a connection there that went beyond the norm, the kind of unconditional love that I couldn't deny, and my chest tightened. Compassion flooded me, and I caught Jason's unflinching blue gaze with my own. He was fiercely protective, and I knew in that instant that he would die for his daughter. Something inside me shifted; from a cop who'd seen too much and a man with a childhood so fucked up it had taken years to come to terms with it, to a primal urge to help keep Daisy safe.

The territorial and passionate feeling blindsided me, nearly took me to my knees, and my breath hitched. Jason calmed Daisy, but she glared hard at me over her dad's shoulder.

So I did what I thought was right, even as Sean moved to finish his checks.

"I'm sorry, Daisy," I murmured. I couldn't let my past color my actions to the point where I'd throw a man against the wall. I was the calm collected one at the precinct, I was steady, reliable, and I didn't let the acid that burned inside me out for any reason.

So what was it about Daisy that had me losing control?

And why was it that abruptly, for no sane reason at all, I wanted to gather her and Jason into my arms, tell them I was sorry I scared them, and then never let anyone hurt them ever again?

SIX

Jason

_____

"WHY DON'T we get Daisy somewhere so I can check you properly," Sean said, and I reacted to the authority in his voice even though I didn't want to let her go.

"I'm sorry," Leo murmured. I'd never seen so much passion and violence in one expression as when he'd shoved me against the wall, and the pain in his expression wasn't something I was going to forget in a hurry.

I didn't even want to think about what he'd seen in his career, but I respected that Daisy was his priority in this situation. None of this was about me, and I didn't care about *me*. I just needed help for my daughter.

"It's okay," I replied to him, and then I tilted Daisy's chin so she'd meet my gaze. "It's okay, Daisy. He won't hurt me."

"I don't like it," she said, and her lip trembled.

"I don't either," I pressed his nose to hers. "Love you forever, Daisy-May."

"Love you too," she replied without hesitation.

"How about you go and play with some things, and

then Doctor Sean can check me out." My voice was shaky, but I pushed as much enthusiasm into it as I could.

"I have some things to play with," Leo pointed, and I looked from him to the front room where a corner was a colorful mess of kids toys. I didn't want to let Daisy go, hell, part of me didn't want to be alone with Leo, and I felt stupid even thinking that. Instead, I settled Daisy with the toys, waited with her for a few minutes as she investigated a plastic treehouse that came complete with an entire family of hedgehogs.

"I can play with any of it?" she asked me, wide-eyed.

I picked up the nearest hedgehog, which was dressed in little dungarees and with a builder's cap, and held it out to her.

"This is Bedge-Hog," I thought on my feet. "He's the one who built the house."

"Bedge-Hog," she repeated the name, and after a moment's hesitation, she took the tiny toy from me.

I picked up another, this one in a pink tutu. "And this is his friend, Lulu."

She glanced up at me. "I can have *both* of them to play with?"

"Yep, all of them if you want," I reassured her as my heart splintered in my chest. Rain had promised that she'd give our child everything, but what had Daisy had? Pain, anger, and a mom who'd lost her way.

"Jason?" Sean asked from the door. "Can I check you out now?"

I ignored him and spoke to Daisy. "You can play with Bedge-Hog and Lulu, and I'm going to talk to the doctor, is that okay?"

She held the two toys to her chest and nodded.

"I won't be long." I noticed Leo's black dog sidle closer, his nose twitching, his tail wagging, but in that super-slow cautious kind of way. To my knowledge, Daisy didn't have an issue with dogs, not that I knew a lot about my daughter. However, she reached out to touch him, and he lay down next to her with a contented sigh and consented to have his silky ear stroked.

They say dogs know things, and I genuinely felt at that moment that he was looking out for Daisy. I just wanted his owner to trust that I was doing the best I could and that we needed help.

Then it was time for me to get my check over from Sean, a proper one.

"You need to get to the hospital for an x-ray," he announced.

"No."

"Stupid," Sean muttered.

All the time Sean was checking me, Leo was observing, hovering at my side with a considering gaze, and his eyes filled with something that I could only class as concern, maybe with an edge of pity? Others might have called it compassion, but I knew he probably saw a man who was less than him, someone who'd allowed themselves to get hurt, a person who lacked control in their life.

I shouldn't have done that, he'd said after the kiss, words that I would never forget.

"He needs an x-ray," Sean said for the third time, although he was talking to Leo and not me.

"I don't," I said, forcing that single word to sound at least halfway lucid.

I needed to pull myself the fuck together and make a

stand, then ask to wait for Eric so he could help me leave. They might try to stop me, but they couldn't. I'd done nothing wrong, and Leo had no grounds to arrest me. Sean had given Daisy the all-clear, although his eyes were filled with questions. Sean was controlled and utterly focused as he asked me questions about my injuries, while I remained silent and didn't tell him a goddamned thing. Leo, on the other hand, was visibly concerned, wavering toward pity, then back to uneasy.

"I'm going to take Mia home for a nap," Ash said, and then turned to Sean, "are we good here? Do you need my help with anything?" I saw him and Sean exchange pointed glances.

"No one calls the cops," I said without hesitation.

Sean shot me a look I couldn't decipher, then huffed noisily. "Everything's okay, don't call anyone."

He and Ash exchanged a kiss, a goodbye, nothing more, and then Ash left.

Sean finished the checks, cleaned me up as best he could, stemmed the bleeding with tiny bandages, and shook his head when I winced as he pressed my ribs. "Not broken," he said. "At least I don't think so, but I need you to come into the—"

"No hospital."

"Jesus," Sean muttered under his breath. Then, with me done, and after much huffing on his part, he cornered Leo in the kitchen, talking *at* him rather than with him. Leo locked his gaze on mine over Sean's shoulder.

Leo was a handsome man, taller than me by a good half a foot, dark hair tidy, his bearing straight. He had laughter lines, but I hadn't seen him really smile yet, not even after our aborted kiss. I'd seen him grateful when he'd approached me after the fire rescue, tense when he'd held my hand in the hospital, but then I'd seen him back away from me post-kiss, regretful, disgusted, completely cutting himself off from me.

I'd seen him spitting furious and shoving me against a wall when he thought I'd hurt Daisy. I'd seen him filled with self-disgust after our kiss. But relaxed and happy? Not at all. He would've been the kind of man I'd gravitate to in a club, or at least he would have been in the old days when the *old* Jason was out looking for hookups. He was strong enough to hold his own in life even with a bum leg, determined enough that he was the one calling the shots, but there was nothing about him now that showed he would be helping me.

"In your opinion should we call Family Services?" he asked Sean.

Even though my chest was tight, I waited for Sean to react. I'd already worked out the exit route, and nothing was blocking my way. All I needed to do was play along, stop my body from forcing me to sleep, then grab Daisy and leave. It might not be the cops or a damn hospital, but Family Services would take Daisy somewhere if they thought she wasn't best placed with me, and that would happen over my dead body.

"Daisy seems okay," Sean said. "But what's your gut feeling?"

Leo glanced over at me, where I sat back on that sofa. "That we don't know everything."

"It goes against my training not to take him to the emergency room."

"Does he have a concussion?"

"He's not showing any signs of concussion, but his ribs…" Sean shook his head. "Fucking idiot."

"He came here to see Eric," Leo defended. "I think we give Eric some time to hear him out."

"Okay," Sean agreed, albeit reluctantly.

The two men were having a complicated conversation filled with moments where they just stared at each other, and I interrupted to cut straight to the chase.

"I just need somewhere to stay for a while, get some space between me and… things," I called over.

Sean and Leo checked me out with narrowed eyes.

"Like the people who beat you up?" Sean asked.

"Who are they?" Leo added. "What do they want with you? Will they know you're here?" The questions were softly asked, but I still winced.

"I just need to stay long enough… then I'll go."

"Go where exactly?" Sean asked.

"Daisy and I have family on the East Coast," I lied, keeping everything non-specific.

Sean sent me a look that spoke volumes, very much a statement of *yeah right.*

"Why do you *need* to stay?" Sean asked and then waited for me to answer. I glanced at Daisy and hoped she wasn't paying too much attention to her fucked-up father. But she was propped up next to the dog, holding Bedge-Hog and Lulu as if they were having a conversation. Back at the house, it seemed to me she'd only ever had her two reading books and a couple of stuffed toys, but right there was a dolls' house, a hundred or more hedgehogs all dressed differently, and an entire shelf of books and stuffed toys.

I wanted that for her. I wanted *normal*, whatever that was.

Sean picked up his cell and turned it over in his hands, his expression thoughtful. "I need to…"

Leo reached out and touched his hand, took the phone from him and thumbed through his contacts. "Daisy is okay, let me look into this, talk to Eric, first," he interrupted.

"Child endangerment—"

"My gut feeling is that there's more than we know here, but I've seen this before, and it's not her dad who hurt her."

"You'll take responsibility—"

"Always."

Sean frowned, and I waited to see what would happen next. So much passed between the two men then, a brotherly connection that made me envious.

"Let's try calling Eric," Sean said, and Leo nodded.

I had to trust that it was Eric he was calling, but whoever he was calling didn't answer. He tried another number, got through to someone he put on speakerphone. Whoever it was who answered said that last he'd heard from Eric was that his team were working in steep areas battling hotspots and were worrying about lingering winds. "I have no idea how long he's up there," the man added, and he sounded a long way past concerned. "They've cut off the power, and it's a mess."

Leo glanced at me and then shook his head before answering. "It's okay, Brady, it might be a mess, but you know Eric, he's trained, and he'll be safe."

Brady, the man who was with Eric, I knew him from the ceremony. He and Leo talked for a few moments, and it was surreal because Brady was just about to go out into his yard with his kids and have what sounded like a normal freaking time for a normal freaking family. They talked a little longer, but when the call ended, Leo and Sean huddled by the front door, and Daisy had moved to sit with her back against the wall, Bedge-Hog and Lulu in her hands and a wary gaze set firmly on me, then Leo and Sean.

The two men talked in hushed whispers, but I could tell from their body language that Leo was worried, and Sean was tense. Then, after a short time, Sean relaxed, and it appeared to have been decided not to talk to Family Services. I owed Leo for that.

Daisy climbed onto my lap and burrowed into my neck.

"You smell the same as Daddy-B," she murmured against my skin, then she added tiredly. "I don't like it."

"I'm sorry, Daisy," I replied, just as quietly. I needed a shower, or at least to wash my face, get some new clothes. But, with no money, stuck in San Diego, needing a sanctuary of sorts for both of us, with Billy out there somewhere, and Rain in the hospital, I was trapped.

And worst of all, Daisy was trapped with me.

SEVEN

Leo

———

JASON AND DAISY CUDDLED CLOSE, Daisy falling asleep, and it wasn't long before Jason joined her, or at least he lost consciousness, although Sean didn't immediately rush to his side and demand I called an ambulance. That left Sean and me standing and staring at the man.

"He saved Eric," I said, and I swear that was the tenth time I'd said that same thing. "We owe him—"

"Respect, a chance, the ability to come to us for help? So you said, *Saint* Leo."

I elbowed him in the side. "What's your problem, asshole?"

"It's my job to worry," Sean said.

"No, actually, it's *my* job to worry, that is what I'm paid to do."

"But I get to worry about you," Sean pointed out.

"Whatever," I said, but we fist bumped to let each other know that whatever we said to each other wasn't what was driving our actions. Of course Sean was worried, but I was the cop here, and I knew Sean was right to be concerned. However, that warred with the stupidly protective side of me that wanted to look after Jason and Daisy.

"I'm trained for this, you know," I reminded him.

"Trained for an ex con with a possibly kidnapped child to land on your doorstep covered in blood?" Sean was incredulous.

"But I've got…" I rubbed my chest. "Something in here tells me that we should take this slowly and that I can handle it. Okay?"

Sean cursed under his breath. "Okay, but somewhere out there is the person who beat up Jason." Sean touched his own throat, "Did you see the marks on his neck, I don't want to say someone tried to strangle him but… Jesus… and the cuts are superficial, not a knife, maybe just from being beaten." Sean had put tiny bandages on each cut, enough to stem the seeping blood, and had finally let Jason sit down, just before the injured man had shut his eyes and his breathing deepened. "The one on his neck, though? It's infected, so I've left some antibiotics, but really? What the fuck?"

"I'll get him to talk."

"This could be a classic case of child abduction."

"I don't think so." I was convinced it wasn't that, but I didn't entirely know why. "I did all the right checks. There's no Amber alerts or open cases. And somehow, I know…"

He knew me too well, I might not have made it obvious, but damn right I'd checked the reports, and there was nothing about a man or a missing kid. He was a first responder the same as me, seeing all kinds of hell in the emergency department of Soledad Hospital, but he also had instincts the same as me, honed by everything we'd seen.

Sean frowned at me, and then the frown turned to sympathy, and abruptly, I knew where this was going. He'd start talking about my childhood, at least the childhood I'd had before I'd been adopted. I was *so* not going there, and I'd definitely not pinned Jason against a wall because Daisy had arrived with blood on her, and it brought back memories of my past. Or of any case involving children.

Who am I kidding? I'd been badly and uncontrollably triggered.

Sean raised an eyebrow, and without saying a word, he'd thrown sympathy at me, along with a healthy dose of understanding, acceptance, and a small amount of sarcastic what-the-hell.

Sometimes having best friends who knew parts of the real you sucked. It was a good job he and Eric didn't know *everything.*

"So, you did all the checks?" Sean asked again.

"Yes, I did, and there's nothing that ties Jason to any crime that I can see on the surface. There was a stabbing in Cove, three shootings in Bird Rock, two robberies on Fifth that could be connected, a violent carjacking on the city limits, a couple of house break-ins. Still, other than that, the last seventy-two hours have been nothing but the usual."

"Jason and Daisy need somewhere to stay," Sean said, and caught my gaze, waiting for me to agree instantly.

I was going to offer Jason and Daisy a place to rest; of course I was. I tried to be a good man and channel what I'd learned as a child. I tried my hardest to care for other people, but there was something about Jason that had me all confused, and even with an injured man and his daughter, I wondered if it might have been better if they went back with Sean.

Why?

Was it because when I'd met him at that hero event at the station I'd been attracted to him? Who even does that? What kind of cop finds a convicted man sexy? Or was it because I'd seen a man that day who didn't want the limelight? Maybe it was because of his sapphire eyes, full of mystery? He was dangerous to me in more ways than I wanted to list.

Whatever my God taught about compassion and love, I was a cop as well, and sometimes "black and white" was just that.

He was an ex-con in my house, bleeding and stinking like week-old garbage, and God knows what, clutching his little girl as if we were going to snatch her from him. What had he done to deserve being beaten? Why was this the first I'd heard about a daughter? I'd researched him—the wrong side of the tracks, brilliant mind, excelled in computer skills, turned to hacking at a young age, family in Seattle. He'd been a drummer in an LA-based band, on the verge of making something of himself and turning away from the hacking, and then he'd admitted to a crime that, in context, made absolutely no sense.

I pinched the bridge of my nose. "This is still partly Eric's house." In fact, he owned fifty percent of it and was the majority holder, with the other half split equally between Sean and me. "He would want us to offer Jason a place to stay, and if you're giving him a medical all-clear…?"

Sean sighed. "Pathologically, there is nothing to suggest he needs to visit the ER. Mentally he's on edge, add in Daisy, and the fact that he's scared and is begging for help, and you have a mess here that, in my opinion, is more a police matter than a medical one."

"Agreed."

"But, Daisy, she might need a different kind of help, counseling maybe, we shouldn't leave this."

"Do you know anyone we can trust?"

He was serious as he thought things through. "I have a couple of options. Let me think about this."

"Okay."

"Also, shit, you should watch him, Leo, and not let… *things*… affect how you deal with this."

He gave me a familiar look, the one that only Eric and I knew best, the one that never judged but silently encouraged us to be better people. Then it seemed as if he took my silence as motivation to keep talking, persuading, pushing me to see a different slant to this situation.

"I won't let *things* affect how I deal with this," I lied. After all, the start I'd gotten in life, and being adopted into the Byrne family, was what had made me the man I was today. "Eric will want us to look out for them."

"Eric is a soft-hearted teddy bear who would give anyone a home," Sean pointed out, but I was aware that I too was a teddy bear where Jason and his small daughter were concerned. So much for a hardboiled cop.

"Yeah, but Eric would also *listen* to Jason, give him some time to explain what the hell is going on."

Sean crossed his arms over his chest, "Yeah well, Eric's an idiot who walks into fires, so why would you even think of following his example."

"Says the one who talked down an active shooter in his ER."

"I was just doing my job," Sean said with a smirk and a wink. "Eric walks into fires, you eat donuts, and I'm just a goddamn all-around hero. Anyway, you're an ass."

I rolled my eyes dramatically. "If I'm an ass, what does that make *you*?"

Sean blinked at me, then smirked. "An ass's friend?"

"Eric *would* offer him a place to stay," I said again after a pause. "The man saved his life, and I won't turn him away."

We both glanced at where Jason was curled up on the sofa, Daisy snuggled into him. She had her eyes open and was looking at both of us, her little hands tightly curled into Jason's shirt. She wasn't letting go, and what would it serve for me to take them anywhere to ask questions? Who would that help?

You, my subconscious argued. *It would help you because you're a cop who should follow the letter of the law*. I glanced at the ceiling as if I could find answers there.

"Not sure praying is going to help here," Sean pointed out, and I elbowed him. "What are *you* going to do?"

"He could stay with you. I'm a cop, and maybe I shouldn't have a convicted criminal in my house." *Particularly one I'm attracted to and who at the moment is confusing the hell out of me.*

"You recall this week's random home visit, right?" Sean said and raised a single eyebrow, Sean-speak for *that is so not going to work*. He had a point—Family Services was arriving at some random time for a home visit part of his and Ash's ongoing journey to adoption. There was nowhere for Jason and Daisy to go, and why was I even questioning this. It was either calling someone or sucking it up and being the good guy.

I am a good guy.

I looked from my friend to Jason and Daisy, and my conscience tweaked, but I couldn't help the insistent poke of trust I was somehow feeling, alongside sympathy. Instinctively, I knew the black and white of the situation, but a small part of me needed to be happy dealing with the gray areas for tonight, or at least until Eric came home.

"I'll make up your old room for them," I sent up a silent wish that I wasn't doing the wrong thing. "But we need to get Eric involved as soon as we can."

"You want me to stay over in case you can't handle it?" Sean asked, completely expressionless, and that got him the biggest shove toward the door.

"I am perfectly capable of handling one weird beat-up guy and his itty-bitty daughter. Out. Go do all that kissing shit with Ash." I added a gagging sound and saw the blank expression turn into a smile at the mention of his husband's name.

"You're just jealous," Sean said with a wink and sauntered away from the front door. I gave him the finger, and he snorted when he saw it. "So jealous."

I was good at that. Making others smile. And yeah, I was a tiny bit jealous. So sue me.

I caught him before he left. "Wait, you never said, how did today go? With the agency?"

He nodded as if that was an answer, then found his tongue. "Good. It's all good."

"If you need anything…"

He pretended to misunderstand my offer of anything

that could mean he and Ash were able to adopt a huge amount of kids. "It might help if you threaten all of the staff at Family Services with parking tickets if they say no." He blinked innocently.

"Bye, asshole," I said, and shut the door in his face. "Who needs friends…?"

I turned to see Jason standing a few feet behind me, Daisy beside him, holding his hand, with his bag hoisted over his shoulder, looking like he was about to go.

"Stay. You need to eat and I have pizza," I blurted before Jason could explain why he thought he and Daisy needed to leave. "Well, what I mean is, I can order pizza." I went down to Daisy's level as best I could with my cast, and she confronted me with that stubborn chin tilt again. "What do you like on your pizza?"

"Peppomi and much-rooms," she murmured after checking with her dad, who nodded at her.

"Okay, pepperoni and mushrooms, it is." Then I stood. "Jason?"

"I'm not hungry," he said, but I saw the way his hand rested on his pocket, probably an automatic move for his wallet, and I doubted that he had any money to his name. After all, he'd come here looking for Eric and a place to stay.

"My treat," I said, and turned my back to them, pulling the menu out of the drawer. "I have coupons," I lied. "I know you can order online, but something is reassuring about a printed menu to show you what you can have. Right?" I turned to face him again and caught his nod, but he didn't give the menu more than a passing glance.

"I'll have the same as Daisy."

Was it the whole like-father-like-daughter thing, or was

he making things easier for me? I wasn't going to argue, because right now there was a more pressing issue.

"Okay, I'll order in a bit. Meanwhile, let me give you these," I handed over a tub of cookies which Mama would be horrified at before dinner, but Jason looked dead on his feet. "Take them for snacks. It will keep you going until I order pizza." I handed Jason two bananas as well, which he balanced on the box. "I'll show you the room you can use tonight. I'm guessing you'd like Daisy in there with you? It's a big bed, you can make a pillow fort for her, or I can drag in the sofa bed from Eric's old room?"

I limped past him to the stairs and gave him the opportunity to escape through the front door if he decided to. Not that I'd let him go, or at least I'd follow him. He needed me; I could see that.

"You really want us to stay?" he sounded confused, and I knew then that he'd decided he was leaving. I wouldn't give him a chance to think he had to go.

"Eric would want you to stay, and until he can get here, you have a bed and a safe place to stay, so let's go."

I climbed the stairs awkwardly and guessed they could follow or not. I pretended to myself that I didn't care, but when I heard their steps behind me, I felt more in control of all of this. The second bedroom with its attached bathroom had once been Sean's, it still had a king bed and furniture, but no bedding. I watched Jason place his bag on the floor, but he didn't let go of Daisy's hand. So I began to elaborate, anything to make them feel more comfortable.

"I'll dig out sheets and stuff. Meanwhile, there's a bathroom there," and then I rattled the handle to the whole room. "You can lock the door if you want, but first, let me get you some stuff."

I headed for my bedroom, dug out sweats and a T-shirt, razors, soaps, found the bubble bath that I kept for Mia if she was there, then fresh towels, and took the whole lot back to the room, placing it all on the bed.

"When you come down, I'll call for the food, so no rush, okay?"

Jason followed me to the door, said a quiet thank you, then shut and locked it immediately.

That was it then, I had house guests, a confused messed-up guy, a frightened little girl, I couldn't get in touch with Eric, and the cop in me was on high alert.

So much for a Sunday where nothing happened.

EIGHT

Jason

I LEANED back on the locked door and slid down the wall to sit. Daisy copied me, cross-legged, and looking a hundred kinds of serious. I'd had everything planned after I'd left prison. I was going to attend any pre-arranged formal meetings that meant I could tick everyone's prisoner-rehabilitated boxes, and I was going to visit Eric and ask for a contact number for his cop friend Leo. I was going to tell him to his face that he could take his regretful kiss and shove it, and that ex-con or not, I was worth everything, and I was a man with a purpose.

Then when I was done with all that, I'd planned on heading for Vermont and the small town of Hill Valley where I thought Daisy had been living a wonderful life with her mom, Rain. Nothing was going to prevent me from going.

Until the FBI had stopped me the morning I was leaving prison.

I had it all planned, Eric, mess with Leo, get signed off by whoever said I was free, find my daughter, start a new life, maybe go to college? Get away from computers, maybe train to be a mechanic, take up drumming again for a small local band. I'd clung to the concept of life on the East coast, where seasons were a thing, and where leaves turned to russet and gold in fall.

Not like here in San Diego, where a hot October had slid into a slightly less hot November without so much as a whimper, and with forest fires still threatening California. I'd grown up on the West coast, lived all my life in the heat of the Californian summers, seen the worst of the wildfires, and the droughts. I'd spent my share of weekends on the beach, though, which was one good thing, but now I needed the opposite of all of that. A cool, calm, silent place where I could remake myself all over again and get involved in bringing up Daisy.

I didn't think I'd be begging for help from someone I didn't know very well.

"Are we staying here, Daddy?" she asked, with every ounce of her nearly four-year-old self in the words. She was worried and looking to me for answers I didn't have.

I wish I had them.

"For a while, I think. It's nice, right?"

She thought for a moment. "I like the toys," she offered as if she knew I needed to hear something positive.

I had to get some help for Daisy, I didn't know what she'd seen, but a counselor who was an expert in children was on my to-do list now. Even though Hill Valley, Vermont, was still on my to-do list, it was way down, for after I got Daisy to safety and helped her come to terms with everything.

But for now, I could at least breathe. We'd been given

a room in a house where Billy wouldn't be able to find us. With a cop.

A cop who'd once gotten carried away with gratitude for me saving his friend. A cop who'd kissed me to stop me arguing, and then stepped back and looked at me as if I was something from the gutter.

Who am I kidding, right now, I am in the gutter.

"Then I think we will stay, and make a proper nest for you to sleep in."

"I'm not a bird, silly," she said, and I saw her smile.

I loved it when my baby smiled at me without shadows in her eyes. I squawked at her, then made a beak with my fingers and poked her belly softly. She laughed then and scampered up to stand by the bed.

I cracked my neck and glanced around the room. There was the big king-sized bed, made of solid wood, with a thick mattress, and I could easily make a safe place for Daisy to sleep on there. The large windows on two sides of the room let in a lot of natural light, filtered through gauzy fabric, and everything was a pale blue, from the walls to the thick carpet under my ass. Along with the bed, there were a couple of storage units and two built-in closets. It was the safest place for Daisy right now, and that was all that mattered.

"So, this is our room?" she asked again, obviously needing reassurance.

"Yeah, pumpkin, we're staying right here for now."

"An' then we're going to get a new house, right?"

"Uh-huh. That is what we're doing, but first, how about we get you in the bath, and then I can have a shower when you're done."

With the pink bubble bath in hand, she headed straight

for the bathroom. I followed her, wincing at the pain in my leg, my shoulders, the ache in my head, and the dizziness, then helped her turn on the taps and fill the bath so that the bubbles nearly spilled over the edge.

Daisy was Little Miss Independence, able to have a bath on her own, get cereal on her own, butter toast to the same level as I could. I dreaded to think why she'd learned so many skills, although up until a few weeks ago, I thought she'd had a reasonably stable home life.

Well, as stable as Rain had been able to give her. Until the stolen money ran out, that was—Rain had taken every cent of the quarter million she'd stolen to help her get a new life.

Bit by bit, a hundred here, a thousand there, over the time I'd been in prison, the money had gone. At first she'd done what she'd promised, gone east, bought a place, made a new life, she'd even tried to get clean, but I guess things had gone south fast, money spent on drugs and whatever the fuck she'd thought was necessary. She'd met a guy called Billy, that was all I knew, and as soon as she was down to the last cent, and after Billy had dished out abuse, she'd gone back to her family.

Back to Silas, her father. Daisy's grandfather was one of the most powerful old-monied men in LA, and he'd wielded that power with absolute dedication. I'd tried my hardest to get Rain away, but everything had gone wrong.

"Are you okay, Daddy?"

I glanced in the mirror, seeing her sitting in the bath, bubbles piled on her head, the bathroom fragrant with strawberries.

"Of course, are you?" I rinsed my razor in the sink and waited with bated breath for her answer. The mirror above the sink was steamed up, but I could shave by feel alone—amazing what skills a man picks up in prison. With each trace of my finger over hairless skin, I felt less like the old Jason who'd fucked up again, and more like a man with a modicum of hope.

"Yep," she said, and I smiled at her, hoping to hell she wasn't astute enough to see through the fakery.

There was the longest pause, some splashing, and then I caught her small voice again.

"Daddy?"

"Yes?" Daisy always had a million questions, but I was careful to answer every one of them because I wanted her to know she mattered in this world.

"Can I have a puppy?"

"A puppy?"

"At our new house."

"Absolutely." I'd promise her the world, and I would try my hardest to deliver on my words.

"And a kitten?" she added, hopefully.

"Won't the puppy and kitten chase each other?" I smiled again.

"Jus' a puppy then," she decided. "And a Christmas tree, because it's Christmas soon? And my birthday an' I'm gonna be four."

My stroke faltered at the endless hope in my daughter's voice. I don't know what she'd seen, but I'd assumed that Rain had given her normal things like birthdays and Christmas. "Yep."

I'd assumed too damn much, it seemed.

"Yes, a puppy and presents and a huge yard where you can play, and you can make friends at school, and we can be a family."

"And can I get my own Bedge-Hog and Lulu?"

"Of course."

She smiled at me, and my heart broke all over again, which was the exact moment my burner phone vibrated. I took it out of the bathroom, wiping my face on a towel as I walked, and answered after the third ring.

"Are you okay?" the caller asked. Austin, a federal agent and both savior and destroyer of my entire damned life. It had been Austin who'd given me the damn phone, so I knew he'd be able to trace this call, and I was damn sure he knew where I was by now. But he hadn't come to get me. Instead, he'd called me, and I was grateful for that, as much as I could be. He sounded troubled, but it was a bit late for concern because he'd once told me everything was going to be okay, and he'd been wrong. It didn't matter if Silas was in custody, no one had thought to watch Rain, or look out for Daisy, or keep Billy off my back.

"We're safe," I said.

"It's fucked up," Austin murmured. "Why didn't you come to me?"

I let out a mocking huff and a curse. "You think I'd bring my daughter anywhere near you?"

Austin's tone softened a little, "I'm sorry, Jason." He wasn't the hard-ass that people thought, and even though he wanted to bring Silas to heel, he wouldn't knowingly put Daisy in danger. "How is Daisy?"

"She's scared, exhausted, doesn't fully comprehend that her momma is in the hospital in a coma, is petrified that someone will try to kill me again and take her, and is scared to death of having to go back to Vermont with Billy."

There was a long pause, long enough that I knew

Austin was thinking things through, or maybe seeking advice from someone.

"You've done your part. Silas is awaiting sentencing, and we'll find Billy and put him away for what he did to you. Stay where you are, keep your head down, it will be over soon."

"How soon?"

"Soon. I promise you."

Great fucking non-answer right there. Pretty much what I'd come to expect from the guys who were attempting to dismantle Silas' operations in Cali, which included drugs, human trafficking, and a whole hell of shit that I wanted Daisy away from. I could've asked for specifics, but I didn't want to prolong the conversation, couldn't bring myself to talk to him anymore. I ended the call before he could, and sat for a moment staring at the handset.

"Daddy?" Daisy called.

"Coming." I headed back into the bathroom, picked up the washcloth she'd lost out of the bath, then concentrated on finishing shaving, gently clearing the scruff from the covered cuts and bruises, knowing the wounds would bleed, but desperate to get the dirt gone. I splashed my face, and when I glanced up, Daisy was leaning her hands on the side of the bath, her chin resting on them.

"Mummy won't be able to come with us to our new house with the puppy and the Christmas tree, will she?" she asked.

I'd promised myself when I'd left the hospital, scooped up clothes and a stuffed dragon for Daisy, that I would be as honest as I could with Daisy, but how could I explain to her that her momma was in a coma, and they'd told me she might never wake up?

"I don't think so," I was as evasive as I could get away with being. I wasn't even sure how aware a nearly four-year-old was where death was concerned.

"It's okay, Daddy, don't be sad, she's happy sleeping, cos when she was awake she was always crying," Daisy observed, sounding more grown-up than her nearly four years would typically be, and then she stood, head-to-toe in bubbles, and I wrapped her in a towel and set her on the floor. She seemed so matter-of-fact about Rain, but I couldn't help but think that she didn't comprehend the full consequences of it all, and the weight of the explanation was heavy on me.

"I know, pumpkin."

She reached over to pull the bath plug, and then padded out to the bedroom. "Imma get dressed," she announced. "What you gonna do?"

"I'll get a shower," I replied, and we grinned at each other.

She looked so much like my sister right then, at least as I remembered Susie from when we were kids before I fucked everything up. I doubt Daisy would ever know her Aunt Susie or her grandparents, and my heart broke for her, but I couldn't drag them into all of this shit.

I took the key with me, left the bathroom door slightly open if Daisy needed me, and showered as fast as I could.

The water was hot, the soap washed away the grime, and by the time I went back out to the main room wrapped in a towel, I felt halfway-human, albeit shaky, lightheaded, and with spots of blood on the pale blue towels. Two cookies later, I felt less like I was going to pass out.

Dressed, I almost felt as if I could take on the world. Or at least one small daughter who had a whole list of questions.

The sweats that Leo lent me were loose, but then Leo was taller than me and more solid around the waist, but I managed to cinch them enough to hold them up, which was a good thing because I had no underwear, given I'd washed my only pair of briefs in the sink and hung them on the shower bar to dry. Hopefully, they would dry quickly enough, but I had to think about what Daisy and I needed just to live. The rest of my things, the jeans, the shirt, they were beyond help, but a visit to Goodwill could be in my immediate future, hell I might splurge on brand new boxers as well if I could get them for a couple of dollars somewhere. I also needed a job, something that paid cash, and at least some kind of focus on where I was going next. I'd promised Daisy a puppy, our own yard, and a Christmas tree, for God's sake.

I'm living in fucking cloud cuckoo land.

At least Christmas was still a month away, not to mention Daisy's birthday on the twenty-third, so I pulled up all the hope I could muster and promised myself that I could make things work by then. Who knew? Austin had used the evidence I'd dug out from Silas' computers to close their case. I doubt Daisy's grandfather would get out of prison for a very long time. Now, all they needed to do was track Billy down, then Daisy and I would be free to go a lot sooner than the weeks he'd initially promised me.

The shirt I pulled on was faded and worn; the irony of the SDPD logo on the front didn't escape me. Two months ago, when I walked out of the correctional facility, I vowed I'd have nothing to do with the cops again and look at me now.

Staying in a cop's house, wearing a cop's clothes, begging for a cop's charity.

"I need you to keep what happened to Mummy and Daddy-B a secret between us, okay?" I didn't like the word Daddy anywhere near Billy's name, but that was what Daisy called him, and I had to live with it for the moment. A big part of me hoped she'd forget him altogether, although how likely that was I didn't know. My memories from when I was four mainly consisted of playing in the park near our house, of the sunshine, and endless days of messing about in the creek that was more often dry than wet. I hoped that what Daisy would remember from being four was that I'd done everything to keep her safe and I was always there for her.

She side-eyed me and gave me a *duh* look that was way too old for her years. "I won't say," she murmured, then she leaned into me and laced her little fingers with mine. "I don't wanna see him again."

"You don't have to," I said with force. "Never again."

A knock on the door interrupted our fierce little circle, and Daisy jumped so high that she knocked my shoulder and yelped.

"Guys? You want me to order pizza now?"

Daisy nodded and rubbed her belly.

"Please," I called back, and then we couldn't hide up there any longer. I balled up my dirty clothes and shoved them into a plastic bag, taking it down with us, and locating Leo in the kitchen, his back to us as he fiddled with a bag of lettuce.

"It'll be here in thirty," he said, without turning. "Can I get you a drink of anything?"

"Water is fine, thank you," I answered for us both.

Leo tipped the final bits of salad into a bowl, then opened his fridge and stared inside. He pulled out a bottle and placed it in front of me, but he didn't bring anything for Daisy yet.

"I have chocolate milk; would you like some if your dad says it's okay?" He spoke directly to her, and I felt her shimmy a little on the high stool. I put a hand behind her just in case, but she seemed steady enough for now.

"Yes," she murmured, and I did the parent thing where I leaned in and prompted her with a whispered *and*? "Thank you," she added and threw me one of her patented Daisy looks that never failed to make me smile.

By not saying anything, I thought I was giving tacit agreement, but Leo stared at me and waited.

"That's fine," I said, and he gave me a half-smile.

If only he weren't a cop.

If only I could trust him.

NINE

Leo

———

WE ATE the pizza pretty much in silence. I was used to having Mia at the table who would babble nineteen to the dozen. Unlike Mia, who was a bundle of energy, Daisy ate slowly, and carefully, and didn't say a word. There was no sign of that stubborn chin tilt or anything like the confidence I'd seen in her when she'd shouted at me. Although every so often she looked at me, sometimes she glared, other times she just seemed confused.

Confusion, glaring, quiet? I could sympathize.

I don't recall the day the Byrne family had picked me up. I was only six, and my head had been too full of memories of the things I'd seen and done. All I knew was that one moment, I was in the foster home, and the next I was the second adopted child of the Mr. and Mrs. Byrne, and that everything was overwhelming. Pulled into the family, an Italian catholic mama, and a former New York cop as a papa, everything changed for me overnight.

But, Mama liked to remind me of how quiet I'd been in the weeks after.

I was a child who was scared for my life and I'd had a lot more to worry about than chatting with a weird kid called Reid who'd said he was now my older brother, or to a woman who'd kept trying to feed me, or a man who'd insisted that I must be respectful. I hadn't wanted an older brother or food, or to be polite. I'd wanted to scream and shout and rail at the world, but it was all caught up in my head, trapped there behind the fear, and it stayed there for a long time.

Until they'd adopted their third child and Jax with his dark red hair and his wide-eyed confusion had landed on our doorstep. Then it had been my turn to be the brave one; to tell him everything was okay, and that he needed to accept he had big brothers and that he should eat everything our mama made, and yes, he needed to be respectful.

Somehow in the craziness of that big family, with so many cousins it was difficult to keep count, I'd lost that mess in my head, and the silence had lessened. It had never gone away. I wasn't as loud and confident as Reid, or always smiling like Jax. When Lorna arrived, the final addition, the only girl, I'd found my place in the family. I'd found a God that seemed to like me, a family that wanted me, and I absolutely remembered the years when my heart began to heal.

But Daisy, sitting here all quiet and concentrating hard on her food, was a couple of steps behind that. Despite her infrequent outbursts fueled by confidence, she was still a little girl who was cuddled right into her dad's side. I was confused, because was she asking for comfort, or was she dealing it out?

As for Jason, he'd said a few words when I'd asked

direct questions, the range of which was from how he liked the food, to the recent San Diego weather. No one could call him a conversationalist, nor me for that fact.

"I have some ice cream," I announced when we'd finished, as I collected the plates to put in the dishwasher. I heard some whispering behind me, but I didn't turn around to check; they probably needed the alone time to make sense of things.

"I think we're just tired," Jason said. "If it's okay with you, we're going upstairs."

It was only six p.m., but I nodded. "I'll be down here if you want to come back and talk," I offered him the chance, but I knew inside that he wasn't coming back down. "You can stay as long as you need," I added.

He wouldn't meet my eyes, then he and Daisy left. I finished clearing the kitchen, rang Brady to shoot the breeze because I knew he missed Eric, and we discussed how quick the fires were spreading. Pictures of burning structures were all over the news, vineyards silhouetted against the scarlet and gold of flames, and candid shots of exhausted firefighters. It was unseasonably warm, and Cali was stuck in a cycle of fires, but neither of us said that out loud.

Eric would be okay.

He had to be.

I didn't push for more. I could hear the nerves in Brady's voice, the worry after what had happened to Eric just a few months before.

Then I was at a loose end, and all the intrigues I had going on in my head compounded until I couldn't help myself. I Googled all the names I had, the ones from the official file on Jason, which didn't hold much more than the name of the company he'd worked for, and what he'd done. He'd pleaded guilty to being part of a money-laundering scheme, removing evidence, which was a federal crime. The sentence had been what I'd expected, but there was nothing officially about why he'd decided to go with guilty or evidence that he'd fought his case at all. There were no lawyers of note involved, just court-appointed representation, nothing that made me think he'd given evidence for a lesser crime. To get more detailed information, I'd have to check out the case at the precinct, maybe call in a few favors.

"Why?" I asked the freezer as I rooted about for the ice cream and pulled out a carton of Rocky Road with a triumphant *yes*, along with a fist pump. I was going to have to walk a marathon to work off the sugar, but for now, it was exactly what I needed. When I went to bed, with the house locked up, Cap took up his place on the landing. It used to be he'd lie there so he'd know where his three favorite men in the world were, but now he did it to watch out for me, or at least I liked to think so. I bent down and scratched his ears.

"Keep an eye on them," I whispered, and he bopped my nose with his own, before turning in tight circles and lying down with a familiar and heavy, put-upon sigh.

And then, with my watch showing a little after ten p.m., there was nothing else for it but to go to bed and carry on with one of the latest spy thrillers in the box of books that Eric had left with me when he'd moved out.

I read for ten minutes, but a book that would typically suck me in failed to keep my attention. When I reread page seventeen for the fourth time, I inserted the business card I was using as a bookmark and closed the novel.

I knew sleep would be a long time coming; I was on edge, waiting for movement, signs that my houseguests were leaving, anything that meant I wasn't doing my job right.

Being a cop meant I was protective of Daisy with her sassy bravery that morphed into prolonged silence and by extension, her dad, who was the opposite of calm.

It's just because it's my job.

Only the thoughts that whirled in my head weren't about protection. They were more about the intriguing story of a little girl and her daddy. Jason Banks, the man with the expressive blue eyes filled with the same pain and fear I saw in victims every day.

I sighed and turned over, my leg aching, my back hurting, and I decided right there that I needed to think about something else; otherwise, I would never get to sleep. I tried relaxing every muscle, from my neck to my big toe, and all the groups in between. I attempted to still my breathing, and I must have finally slept, because I'd never had a waking nightmare as visceral as the one that dragged me awake, sweating, and panting.

I'd been sprinting towards some unknown *thing* in the nightmare, never quite reaching where I wanted to go before someone died, and adrenalin pumped around my body with my heart beating overtime. It was one a.m., for God's sake, and I'd had very little sleep, and my head was spinning. I didn't have to visit a counselor to know that there was a shit ton of unresolved mess inside me. I kicked out the covers which had tangled around my feet, before falling back onto my bed and staring at the ceiling.

"So, it's like this." I began to talk in a soft murmur, not even caring if God was listening, or even if anyone else out there in the cosmic wild cared. "I was on a call, and I don't know how to process what I saw, and I know I've talked about this before, but you need to know it's messing with my head."

No one said anything back, and there was no silent press of a hand to my arm in reassurance, it was just me and the silence of a San Diego night, so I kept talking.

"I went to a women's shelter we'd been to before, but you know that I guess." I stopped and closed my eyes, part of me not wanting to recall the details of what I'd seen. This was what the counselor wanted me to confront in my head, but I'd told her I was okay, that it was just work. She'd been skeptical, but I'd talked myself through our first session. What I'd seen had pulled up skeletons from a childhood long before I was adopted, but with a broken leg, I would at least get time to breathe at home.

Breathe? Who was I kidding, it was more like one day I would suffocate in repressed memories.

"The woman was dead in the hallway," I continued, recalling the scent of blood and cordite, remembering the bright poster on the wall with a cute dancing telephone and a helpline number. There were toys strewn on the floor, some were the same as the ones I'd gotten for Mia, and I knew then in my gut that there was a kid in there somewhere.

"The man, her husband, was sitting in the corner, right back, his arms around his knees, blood on his hands, and a gun on the floor between them. I guess she'd let him in, and I didn't know what he'd said to get her to open the door, but there it was, she did, and he'd killed her in her room, in front of witnesses. There was a crib, and I swear the little girl in there was no more than Mia's age." I swallowed the instant grief and the fog of memories that threatened to push out from me. My God knew all of this, but he would listen.

I needed someone to listen who'd be able to take everything from me and hold me close for a while.

"I don't question what you do, but she was so tiny, a little scrap of a thing, and her dad was an abuser and murderer, and now her mom is dead. How do I process that, huh?"

Still no answer; there wasn't a sudden chill in the air, nothing in the way of a sign from God, or even the ghosts that lived inside me.

"Her name was Natalie," I continued, and I held out my arms in front of me in the half-dark of my room, imagining here there. "She was a pretty girl, crying continuously, and I didn't know what to do. She didn't react as Mia does; she wasn't happy to be held, and she didn't smile at me."

I sighed heavily.

"So I guess today, I want to ask you to keep an eye on her for me, and to look out for her mom, wherever she's gone. The dad, though? I can't ask you to do anything, but right now, I need to believe there was some reason for all of it, I just can't get there."

I rolled over, pulling my leg with me, wincing at the ache, and tugging the covers over me. Something about talking to my God was cathartic, and for a while, I slept.

TEN

Jason

I WOKE UP, sweating and terrified in the dark, afraid that I'd lost Daisy. Panic gripped me, and I sat upright so fast my head spun, and god, my chest hurt, as if knives were digging into me. Only when I saw Daisy on the other edge of this enormous bed, protected in a pillow fort, did the terror inside lessen. Still, I yanked myself out of the twisted blankets to get to her, cursing at the pain, just to stroke her hair and reassure myself she was here.

My watch showed it was a little after three a.m., and God knows where that time had gone, because despite the terror, as soon as I'd been able to lock us inside this room, I'd slept. Daisy had wanted to watch cartoons on the TV in the corner, but that had lasted all of five minutes, and she was out like a light.

That was my fault.

We'd fled from the hospital three days ago, leaving Rain because there was nothing I could do for her, and Daisy was my first concern. We had nowhere to go, no money, and not much purpose, but all I knew was that we had to get out of Billy's way.

I had to believe that the doctor next door had checked her thoroughly because then I would worry that she was sleeping so much. Maybe I should ask for him to do tests or something? I laid back on the pillows and stared at the ceiling, not being able to make out much more than the blankness in the gloom. The night terrors had left me sticky and uneasy, and I wasn't ready to close my eyes again as my chest grew tighter. Only when my breathing became thready, when I was forcing myself to inhale, the rhythm all wrong, did I get up and out of bed. For the longest time, I stood there, staring at nothing, trying to empty my head of all things awful.

Like standing in the hospital, Rain still in the bed kept alive by feeding tubes. Like Billy sneering at me and telling me there was nowhere he wouldn't find me after what I'd done when I'd betrayed Silas.

Like every shitty fucking thing that had piled on top of me.

Maybe Daisy would wake up? Would she be thirsty? I glanced around for the sippy cup she was using, but couldn't see it anywhere. What kind of dad was I not to bring that upstairs with me?

Restless and worried about the cup, I calculated the risk of dashing downstairs to the kitchen to get it. I should have thought of this before we'd shut ourselves in, but all I'd been interested in was getting away from Leo's assessing gaze. Not quite suspicious, but it was a look I'd seen before, pity mixed with mistrust. I unlocked the door quietly, and checked back at Daisy, making sure she was asleep before I rushed downstairs.

I took one step into the darkness and stepped on Cap, who was *right there*, squirming and yelping. I immediately jumped sideways, so I didn't hurt him and crashed into the door opposite so hard my teeth rattled. I think I shouted, cursed, but all I know is that as I sat there stunned and uncoordinated, the door I had crashed into, the one I was leaning on, was pulled open violently, and I fell back into the room behind. Light burned my eyes, and I covered my face, waiting for the pain, but instead, all I got was some gruff cursing and someone gripping my arm.

"Jesus," Leo snapped and helped me stand. As soon as I was steady on my feet, I opened my eyes, and got an eyeful of a half-naked Leo, brandishing a baseball bat, his hair wild around his head. "What the fuck?" He seemed to think that was going to elicit an answer from me, but where did I even start?

So I said nothing at all and backed my way out of his room. But he dropped the bat and limped the small distance between us, up in my space in an instant, holding my arm, all concerned.

"Jason? Are you okay? Is it Daisy? Is someone here?"

"No, I'm…"

For the longest time, I stared at him in the soft glow of the light from his room, so close I could see his feathered lashes, see right into his eyes, and feel the puff of his breath on my face.

I swayed.

I swear to God, I swayed toward him, let him take the weight off me to keep my balance, and his eyes widened.

"Jason? Talk to me, are you okay?"

Was I okay? That was a loaded question, and fuck knows if I knew what to say. I shrugged free of his hold and backed toward our room, picking my way over Cap, who didn't appear overly offended that I'd trodden on him, and then I locked myself in.

The knock startled me. "Jason? Did you and Daisy need anything?"

Fear gripped me, and I knew it was stupid, but the sippy cup wasn't a priority, and Daisy was sleeping, so right now, all I wanted was for Leo to think that everything was okay.

"No, we're good," I said and cleared my throat. "Is uhm… your dog… is he okay?" I grimaced and rested my forehead against the cool wood of the door. I could have hurt the poor black Labrador, and that was a shitty move.

"Cap's good."

"Good," I winced at repeating the word. I'd hurt myself falling into that door, and my chest was on fire, so words were hard to find right now. I wondered why the dog was called Cap. Was it short for Captain? Who had called it Cap? Had Leo owned Cap since he was a puppy?

Leo with a puppy? I pressed a hand to my chest and closed my eyes. I had no words right now. Hell, it was an effort just to get my breathing straight.

There was the most prolonged pause ever, but I didn't hear him move away, and then I thought I heard a sigh. "Okay then, I meant to say there's cereal downstairs, but I can make pancakes for breakfast in the morning if Daisy wants them."

"Uh-huh."

"Just come down any time you're ready."

I nodded as if he could see me, and then I felt too stupid to say anything, so I went back to the bed and sat on the side, letting my eyes get accustomed to the gloom. My mom always used to say that darkness made every fear and hurt a hundred times crueler than it would seem in daylight. What would she say now if I admitted that the blackness was actually inside of me, and it didn't even go away with sunlight?

"Daddy?" Daisy's voice was sleepy, and she rolled toward where I would've been lying. "Wanna go potty."

I scooped her up into my arms and made my way carefully to the tiny bathroom, switching on the soft light and helping her to go for a pee. I didn't talk to her, as her head nodded against me. She was so grown-up, precocious, and focused, nearly four, her birthday a few days before Christmas. Or at least, that was what Rain had told me. One random night when I'd sought peace in someone's arms, despite all my misgivings, and now I was a daddy.

I wouldn't have had it any other way. From the moment I met her for real only a few short weeks ago, Daisy had become my everything and the center of my entire world.

There were things in my past I'd change, but I wouldn't change *now*, not this moment where my precious child clung to me as I carried her to bed then, with absolute trust that I would look out for her, she fell back to sleep.

"Maybe sleep is your safe place," I whispered, and pressed a kiss to her soft curls. "I wish it was mine."

Instead, I lay back and stared at that ceiling until it was light enough that I could make out a couple of thin cracks, ignored the growing burn around my ribs and my increasingly labored breathing, and concentrated on as many happy thoughts as I could.

I'm not in prison. I can leave any time I want.

I'm not in prison, and when they've found Billy, I can start a new life with my daughter.

No, I wasn't in prison, and Leo had been there ready to fight someone for Daisy and me.

On a shallow note, the insistent thought crept in, that shirtless Leo, with his muscles, the scent of him warm from bed, and the darkness of hair on his chest, looking for all the world as if he could take on a freaking Terminator, was one of the most shockingly sexy things I'd seen in a long time. So shocking that I almost forgot I was supposed to dislike him.

Sleep never happened, and I watched dawn lighten the room.

ELEVEN

Leo

I WISHED I could go for a run because I needed it in a bad way. What had happened with Jason and Daisy yesterday, and then Jason last night, had left me unable to sleep, on top of the fact I'd already lost hours to my internal misery. I'd been worried they were going to leave in the middle of the night before I'd even found out what the hell was going on and why Jason was there. Also, had he hurt himself falling over Cap and careening into my door? Could he be upstairs now in pain?

Not to mention the way he'd subtly moved closer when I'd held him steady. I'd felt the muscle flex under my arm, had seen the way his lips had parted, and for an insane second, I'd really thought maybe I would lean into him until he'd tugged himself free.

Who the hell could sleep after that? I wanted to be first in the kitchen this morning when they woke up. I'd been downstairs since five, and they still hadn't come down, not that I expected them to be up just yet, again, I couldn't help but worry.

I sat at the kitchen table, nursed my coffee, and closed my eyes, attempting to find my peace. Cap pressed against my foot snoring loudly, and I sent up a quick prayer to God to keep my family and friends safe, in particular, Eric again. Then it was all about sitting around and waiting for Jason and Daisy, but I wasn't surprised when one of my siblings phoned a little after seven.

When Lorna called, it was usually because of a boy and always in the evening. Reid had this whole mess at his precinct with a guy who he swore up and down was on the take, but he never called unless it was the weekend. So it had to be Jax, who always managed to touch base with me early on weekdays when he knew I wasn't on duty, to catch up with everything. That was how we'd grown up, always aware of where each other was, probably a leftover from the times we'd been in our individual foster homes. I tried to know where everyone was now, even attempted to instigate a system when I'd lived with Sean and Eric, but of course, they weren't here now, and their lives weren't as snarled up with mine as I wanted, which was unsettling. I was definitely closest to Jax, which made it cool to answer the call, even though he could well ask me how I was, just in conversation, and this morning I felt as if all my worries, fears, and insecurities would spill out without stopping.

"So Reid's not calling me back," Jax blurted instead of his usual cheery good morning.

"And?"

"He's an asshole," Jax muttered, and I relaxed a little as this was clearly not a dangerous emergency but a sibling thing. For some reason, I had become the peacemaker of the four Byrne siblings, and sometimes it sucked, and other times, I felt like the most exceptional negotiator on the planet.

"What did he do?"

"I swear he helped himself to two cans of paint that were in the yard, meant for one of my renovation projects —the good stuff, you know?"

"Okay, what? Reid stole your paint?" It was way too early for this.

"He sure did. I mean, who else would it be? Mama WhatsApp'd me to show off photos of her newly decorated front room and how lucky she is to have a clever son like Reid, and it's the same fucking shade, so it had to be him who took it, right? I mean, you're a cop, you should be able to arrest him or something."

Cap twisted around my legs as I bent to unload the dishwasher. I stumbled up and back into the counter and stubbed a toe on a chair, which freaking goddamn hurt like a mother.

"I'm not arresting one brother, who is a cop, for borrowing paint from another brother, particularly when said original brother did it just to make Mama smile, asshole."

I took the call outside with my coffee, wondering if I now had a broken toe to match my tibia, as I limped. All the while, Jax was talking at me in my ear, and Cap bounced behind me, whining and picking up a Frisbee.

"I'm not playing," I warned Cap, with my hand on the mic.

"Reid needs arresting," Jax grumped, and by the time I made it to the comfortable chair just outside the patio doors, he'd worked up a head of steam about brothers who were assholes. I hoped he didn't include me in that. It was way too early on a Monday morning for a conversation with anyone, let alone the most hyperactive of my siblings, who would not let things lie.

"You need to caution him," he finished his tirade, and I had to hold back the snort of laughter that he was phoning to ask me to abuse my cop powers on our brother.

"Jax, are you more pissed he borrowed your paint—?"

"You can't *borrow* paint!" he interrupted.

"—or are you pissed off that Mama has been asking you to decorate her place for at least a year and you've been too busy? Leaving her to tell me at every given moment how proud she is of you, but also how sad it is that you'd forgotten her?"

Jax huffed, and then cursed, and I knew that I'd hit the nail on the head. Jax ran a hugely successful renovation company, started from nothing, and worked all hours God sent just to keep on top of everything. It used to be he'd help out family, after all, it was projects like painting his bedroom black and yellow, or erecting a room addition to the side when Lorna had joined the family, that had taught him his craft. It was only in the last couple of years he'd become a victim of his own success. It was blatantly apparent that he felt guilty for not helping Mama, and with his OCD for keeping track of the supplies for each job, it was evident that guilt and missing paint had collided to instigate this morning's call. Of course, it didn't help that Mama had this way of making each of her kids feel guilty for one thing and another.

With me, it was a lack of a girlfriend, or boyfriend, or *whatever*. She didn't care which, she just wanted grandchildren, and the five she did have, courtesy of Reid and his lovely wife Rachel, and Jax with his ex, Paula, were clearly not enough to spoil. And boy, were each of her grandchildren spoiled. When my siblings and I were growing up, we were ruled with a rod of iron, along with a healthy dose of Italian cursing. Still, the minute her grandchildren had arrived, they'd been treated to gentle words and unlimited biscotti. She'd softened a little over the years, but I didn't have to look far to find the iron underneath the soft grandkids-loving exterior.

Cap jumped up and placed his paws on the cast iron table next to me, resting his snout on the back of a chair and side-eying me, using every ounce of his puppy power in that soft, velvet gaze. He knew damn well I had a treat in my pocket, and anyone would've thought he was starving.

I covered the receiver with my hand to talk to him. "You seem to think I've forgotten the great opening-the-kibble-yourself caper," I admonished, and he blinked up at me. I tried to harden my heart to his gorgeous bear-like face, but then he let out a low whine, and if anything, he was even cuter and more desperate. And my hard heart melted.

"One," I admonished, and threw a small chew onto the grass, ensuring it would be an adventure for the black lab to find. An adventure he undertook with great enthusiasm, a clatter of paws, and the entire shifting of a vast green bush that quivered as he dived in. "And don't tell anyone."

Not that there was anyone to tell, given I lived alone now. Unless I told Jason or Daisy, I guess.

"Huh?" Jax asked.

Hell, I'd forgotten he was still on the phone and released my hand so he could hear me talking to Cap as if he was a human. "Never mind." I tilted my head to the morning sun, it might have been heading for winter in Cali, but it was still way too warm at seven a.m. "Jax, there's nothing I can do here, chalk it up to the fact Reid clearly wants something from Mama, and is creeping around her to get it, and will likely get a clip round the ear when she realizes she's being played. You know, Mama isn't stupid."

Jax sighed. "He's still an asshole, and I'm counting on you to help me jump him at Mom's for Thanksgiving, okay?"

"Gotta go, Cap has someone pinned at the door..." That was my default excuse, and at the mention of his name, Cap glanced up and gave me a drooling doggy grin. Cap had never pinned anyone anywhere, but to hear me roll out the excuse, anyone could be expected to meet a slobbering attack dog, not a bear of a puppy with a heart of gold and a penchant for Frisbee.

Big celebration days ranged from Christmas and Thanksgiving right down to lesser saints days, and it was a way for the entire family to get together. My parents' house was a sprawling ranch type affair, big enough to house siblings, nieces, nephews, and a multitude of cousins, and attending the special events was a tradition for any of her children who could make it home. Even when I was on duty, I managed to get to every single one for at least a few minutes if I could, but when I was off duty I'd get the full Mama experience, one in which I knew I'd end up rolling home with a belly so full that all I'd want to do is sleep. Thanksgiving was the worst, so much food, and if I added that to the lack of exercise, then by the time I was back at work, I'd end up the size of a hippo.

"I need to get some more exercise in."

I stretched, basking in the early morning sun for a little while, sent a quiet prayer to the heavens for everyone I loved, particularly Eric still up in the hills, and then I went back indoors, an inquisitive black lab right on my heels. I needed to fix breakfast, more coffee, and then see if I could coax Jason and Daisy downstairs.

Forgetting the almost lean-in was my number one priority, and getting a semblance of control back, my second.

Both good intentions flew out of the window when Jason came into the kitchen, Daisy holding his hand. Cap nudged her, and instead of pulling away, she carefully touched his head and patted him gently. He loved that, butting her fingers and then panting like an idiot.

I met Jason's gaze over her head, and for a second, we exchanged small smiles.

I guess kids and dogs did that to a man.

And it was nothing to do with the fact that I *wanted* to smile at Jason.

Not at all.

TWELVE

Jason

———————

I DIDN'T KNOW what had changed since yesterday, but
somehow Daisy and Cap were friends, even though she
remained cautious, and he was respecting her boundaries.

She sat on the floor and fussed over him, as Leo made
chocolate chip and banana pancakes, along with bacon so
crispy it was enough to have me wanting more. Not that I
asked for any, because we were lucky to get what we were
given. I tapped out a rhythm on my leg under the table as I
ate, and it quietened the fears that circled inside me. A
concern that warred with gratitude as he made strong
coffee and offered Daisy milk. He was doing everything to
be the best host.

Was there anything this man couldn't do?

Somehow, he was winning Daisy over, one pancake
bite at a time as he stood at the stove whistling tunelessly
and not asking me about what the hell had happened in the
middle of the night. Cap was under the table, waiting for a
piece of dropped food, no doubt, but even he wasn't giving
me a hard time about trampling him last night. If anything,

he was more interested in Daisy and probably more so in what food she might accidentally on purpose give to him.

Leo's cell vibrated on the counter, and he picked it up and wedged it between his neck and ear, multitasking with the pan and batter.

"Hey… yeah, I know… seriously?" He glanced over at me, but he wasn't smiling, and my stomach fell.

Horror gripped me. Somehow whoever was on the phone had tied my name to Silas, and they were telling Leo that he needed to arrest me and take Daisy away. It didn't matter that I'd done nothing wrong. The rhythmic tapping on my leg became a single steady beat that matched the frantic action of my heart. Leo met my eyes, and he looked so serious, but not angry, or as if he was going to reach for a weapon and separate me from my daughter. If anything, there was a worry in his expression, along with a subtle resignation.

How was it that I thought I could read any of that in his face?

"Okay… yeah…" Leo sighed. "Okay, talk tomorrow," he ended the call and sighed heavily. "That was Brady. Eric isn't due back until the weekend."

Fear and worry flooded me because I knew what it would be like up there, and for a second, I was light-headed, and pain gripped my side. "But he's okay, right?" I recalled whole weeks where we lived and breathed fire, anything to stop it spreading to towns and taking lives. Eric had been a good guy. *Wait, he* is *a good guy; nothing will happen to him.*

"He won't know you're here if that's what you meant." He leveled a look at me that could only be described as accusing.

"I didn't mean that, I—"

"What would Brady say to Eric anyway? It's not as if Eric can stop what he's doing in San Bernardino to deal with whatever you have going on."

Jeez, Leo obviously wasn't all sunshine and positivity this morning.

"He doesn't have to know anything, he just needs to do his work and stay safe," I defended myself.

Leo closed his eyes briefly. "Sorry," he apologized after a while. "I forget that you know… I hate that I can't be up there helping him, even if it's just working admin."

"It's okay. I won't be here long. I don't have money, though…" Leo didn't have to let me stay here; he wasn't Eric. He didn't owe me any help at all.

Leo tossed his phone to the work surface and crossed his arms over his chest. "Are you ready to tell me what's going on yet?"

I didn't know anything about what could happen. I'd pinned everything on Eric being the one to offer Daisy and me a place to stay, with no questions asked. Instead, I was stuck with Leo, and Eric didn't need to know. Was this Leo telling me that we had to leave?

"Please don't make us go just yet," I swallowed my pride. I could sleep on a bench or table-hop at all-night diners, but Daisy needed stability and safety. "Or at least keep Daisy here where I know she's safe."

"I wouldn't make you go anywhere, you're welcome to stay here." He grimaced as he spoke, and I had the distinct feeling that it would have been easier to get him to agree to take in someone from the FBI's Most Wanted list. He gestured at Daisy with the carton of milk, "Anyway, I don't have any choice when there's a child involved, and we owe you."

"You have to promise that you won't tell anyone where I am." Not an easy question to ask a cop when I was a convicted felon.

The Feds didn't know who they could trust, I didn't know who to believe, but I had to have confidence in Leo and his obvious love for his best friend. The only problem was that he was a cop, and his first instinct surely had to be to report us being here and make it official. I'd bet my ass he'd already made his cop colleagues aware of the strange guy who'd turned up at his house with a child in tow, so I needed to know how long I had before Billy found out where Daisy and I were. I examined him, saw the gray smudges under his eyes, and concluded that we'd both lacked sleep last night, and I felt guiltier.

I was good at feeling as if everything was my fault.

"I won't. For now." Leo turned his attention to Daisy and changed the subject. "Did you sleep okay?" he asked her as he joined us and then piled his plate with pancakes, which he'd made adeptly, albeit one-handedly while he leaned on the counter with his other. I couldn't even make pancakes with both hands. He looked at me as he asked, and caught me staring, which I tried to hide by focusing on the coffee in my mug. What was he thinking about? What training had kicked in for him? Had he checked out my name? Was he going to be the one who would take Daisy away even though Austin said she was safe with me? Dread pooled in my stomach, and although I'd done everything they asked of me, I was scared.

"It was a very dark room," Daisy's reply was solemn.

"Would you like a nightlight?" Leo asked, and I stared at him, waiting for him to meet my gaze. *Huh?*

"Uh-huh," she murmured and went back to eating her pancake, in tiny little pieces.

"*If* you stay, then I can find you one of Mia's that I keep here," he added and returned my stare.

If? That didn't sound like he was going to let us stay. "The minute you can't help us, we need to go," I finally managed, and Leo inclined his head, nothing more than a small movement to acknowledge my words. "We *will* go," I added, with force.

"But my nightlight…" Daisy protested.

He still spoke to Daisy. "If your dad says you have to leave, then you can put the light in your backpack and take it home."

With great deliberation, Daisy placed her fork on her plate. "Daddy said I don't have to go home." She stared up at me, tears filling her wide blue eyes. "Right, Daddy?"

My heart.

"That's right, pumpkin," I tried for a goddamn ray of sunshine positivity, even though my heart was breaking for my little girl and the fear in her expression. "We're going to make a whole new home, just for you and me."

She wiped at the single tear which had escaped and nodded. "I don't want to go back to Daddy-B."

"You won't have to. Eat the rest of your pancake, sweetheart."

"I'm all done now," she murmured and leaned into me, and we hugged for a little while until she wriggled free. "Can I go play?" She pointed at the big house with the hedgehogs, and I couldn't force her to eat more or to stay right next to me where I could see her. I tried not to meet

Leo's eyes, but I knew he was staring at me, I could feel the heat of a cop's gaze on my skin.

"If that's okay with Leo," I said, and he nodded.

We watched her go to the playhouse, Cap trailing her and taking his blanket with him, curling up next to where she played, a quiet and focused guard dog, it seemed. From Leo I could feel the weight of unspoken questions I knew he would have, I just didn't expect him to go for the jugular as soon as she was out of hearing.

"Why can't she go home, Jason? Who is this Daddy-B guy?" he asked, and I hunched in on myself, cradling the cooling mug of coffee like a lifeline. "I'm fucking serious here, Jason. Are you even listening to me?"

"Someone her mom was dating," I said, pushing at the nagging pain in my chest with my fist, and finally glanced up at Leo. Big mistake, because he took it as an indication that I wanted to talk.

"What did he do to her to make cry, Jason?"

"Not to her, to her mom," *and me.* I didn't want to see the horror that I was sure would be in his eyes. "She's sad and scared."

"What the hell is she so scared of?"

I concentrated on my breathing, which hurt, and the pain in my head, which hurt even more.

"Not me."

"Then where's Daisy's mom, Jason?"

I hated the way he added my name to the questions, probably something he was taught in cop school as a way of connecting with suspects like me.

Are you going to tell us the truth, Jason?
Will you make a deal with us, Jason?
Can you hide the truth just a bit longer, Jason?

Jason, help us to help you.

"Daisy's mom is in the hospital, in a coma, an overdose, I took Daisy from the hospital to keep her safe." That seemed like a lot to get out in one go, but when I paused, he filled in all the blanks in quick succession.

"You took Daisy from her mom?"

"Rain had overdosed, she's in a coma—"

And then Billy found us, I kept that to myself.

I had to believe that Billy wouldn't find us and that somehow the Feds in general, and Austin particularly, would keep their word and find Billy first.

"We just need a place to stay, that's all."

"You know I'm a cop. I can help you if you tell me what's going on."

"Yes, I know that—"

"Also, that it's my duty to report any crime, irrespective of the fact you saved my best friend's life at great personal risk?"

I wonder what was more real to him; his career or his friendships, or were they so closely entwined that he could never hope to unravel the connections?

"I know," I said, miserably.

"You owe me this much, Jason. Am I in the middle of something that will destroy my career? Or even worse than that, my friendship with Eric, or my family?"

I blinked at him, and the tapping on my leg grew erratic, and I gripped my hand with the other to stop the tic. Of course, everything I was mixed up in could affect him, if Billy knew where I'd taken Daisy, then he'd track me down, and that would put Leo right in the middle of it all. It didn't matter how unlikely that was; it could happen. So what did I do now? He reached for more coffee and filled my mug, then nudged cream and sugar toward me. There was no reason I shouldn't trust Leo with my life because I'd already thrown myself and Daisy on his mercy.

Fuck, way to be so damn dramatic. The Feds know I'm here, they know I will keep my head down for Daisy's sake.

None of that will impact Leo.

"You're not in the middle of anything that can hurt you." I waited for him to react. Only he didn't push for more, nor did he march me into another room, he just sat there and looked at me.

"Then, for now, you're safe here."

I think the bitter caffeine and his reluctant agreement to help the two of us, or at the very least Daisy, lulled me into a false sense of security.

Was it possible that I'd finally get some help for Daisy? Or was Leo playing me with his quiet assurance that I would be safe? What would happen when he talked to the Feds? And how much would they tell him?

He stood to brew more coffee, and I was concentrating so hard on him that I ended up staring at his ass. Not deliberately, but it was right there in my face, right at my eye level, and even as messed up and exhausted as I was, I couldn't help but love the way his sweatpants curved around his butt. At least it was an objective observation, and it was more a focus point to help me think.

Yeah right.

I stood up and pushed my hands into my pockets as if I didn't have a care in the entire damn world. He copied me, and abruptly we were toe to toe, and I tilted my chin so I could meet his gaze. I knew enough to make sure it didn't seem as if I was lying, and for a long time, he just stared at me.

"Thank you," I murmured.

"Okay," he said, but I caught an added "*fuck this*" as he turned away.

THIRTEEN

Leo

"Cap needs a walk," I announced when it seemed that Jason had no more to say, and at the use of the word *walk*, Cap was by my side, Daisy following. "And you need clothes, both of you, and other things I can't even begin to list. But first, let's go to the park."

"Imma get my shoes!" Daisy announced with a grin and scampered out of the room.

"I think we should stay here," Jason began.

I needed to get out, Cap needed a walk, and fuck if I was leaving them here on their own.

"The park is at the end of the street."

"Yeah, but—"

"There's a park, somewhere shady I can tie up Cap and a sports store that has a kids' section, and mostly I need some fucking air, and I'm not leaving you and Daisy here on your own."

Decision made, I dared him to argue, but if anything, he was defeated, and when he'd scooped Daisy up into his arms, slipping his feet into his battered running shoes while awkwardly balancing her, he followed me out of the door and into the midday sunshine.

"I don't have any money," he sounded mortified.

"Eric will cover what you need," I said, and he shrugged at that, beaten down by whatever was going through his head. I settled my weight on my crutches, taking both because I was tired and shaky, and damn it, I was supposed to be the one in charge here. Which of course meant Cap was off the leash, but he was so good, keeping pace with me, right by my side.

We headed for the park, Cap darting here and there as soon as we were inside the gate, anything to run off some of his energy. Daisy asked to be let down, with Jason hovering protectively as she climbed the frame of a slide and giggled as she went down it. He was wary, checking around him, his hands outstretched whenever Daisy was too far out of his reach. He was overprotective, but she didn't seem to mind; if anything, she was happy to hug Jason, and Cap was bouncing all around him, so I was evidently the odd one out on the whole trusting-Jason thing.

Calling Cap, I took him over to the short grass, so he could sniff every blade, and pulled out my cell phone, all the time watching Jason. I only relaxed fully when Daisy was right at the top of the frame, and I knew Jason couldn't run.

I was waiting for him to run, not that I'd be able to do much running after him.

Bella answered on the first ring. "Why is it you can't just have your days off and actually chill?"

"So much for a hello and how are you, Leo?" I huffed a laugh. She'd been my partner for the longest time until she was promoted to a joint task force with the SDFD. Unfortunately, she'd been replaced by Yan, a dim newbie who needed to buck his ideas up if he was going to survive to be a career cop. While I was off injured, he'd been reassigned to someone else, an older cop with twenty years on the street who didn't take any shit, so I just hoped I'd go back to a partner who'd learned from the best.

"Whatever, you're the one sitting at home having a vacation," she teased.

"I wish, anyway, the reason I'm calling is that I want you to check into something for me."

"What is it about the title *former* partner you don't understand?" she teased, but I pictured her with her notepad, pen poised to write, and I knew she'd do anything I asked if it was possible. Same as I would for her.

"Whatever," I deadpanned. "You know you miss me, and I have this possible case, but it could be nothing."

"Then you should call that kid they paired you with," she teased, busting my balls because she could.

"He wouldn't know a case from a backpack," I huffed a laugh and she joined in, but then she sobered.

"Okay, so you want this done on the down-low?"

"Yeah, the person of interest is Jason Banks, just did time in Lowton Correctional, volunteered as a firefighter when he was inside."

"A firefighter, wait, is this *the* Jason? The one who nearly died saving Eric?"

"Yep, *that* Jason." Great, now I felt guilty that I was even doing this at all. I pushed it to one side and focused on anything else that Bella needed to know. "Also, Daisy, not sure of her last name, around three or four years old, somehow connected to Jason. Oh, and a woman, Daisy's mom, name unknown to me, who allegedly is in a coma."

"A coma, jeez, Leo, what the hell have you got yourself into? What hospital is she at?"

"I have no idea."

"I'm guessing San Diego, though?"

"Could be New York or Timbuktu for all I know."

Bella snorted a laugh. "Helpful. So what am I looking for?"

"I honestly have no idea."

"But, you're looking into this for Eric, right?"

"Totally Eric, not a favor for me at all."

"Talking of tall, dark, and sexy firefighters, is Eric still taken?"

I huffed a laugh, Bella had this *thing* for my friend and had been so disappointed when he'd gotten with Brady until of course she'd seen them together and explained that it even softened her cop's heart to see them in love.

Cap tugged on the lead, and I scratched his head, "Very much taken."

"Dammit. Okay, so, Jason, Daisy, and a connection, you have no idea what you're looking for. And you want it just between us, okay?"

"Thank you, Bella."

"Always."

After ten minutes of Daisy playing, and watching Jason move slower with each passing moment, I decided to cut to the next part of this trip. The sports store was one of three outlets, one covered alternative foods, for want of a better description, and the other a yoga studio. Never let it be said that this area wasn't catering to a particular kind of resident. I tied Cap up in the shade, next to the bowl of

water that had been left out by the hooks in the wall, and
then awkwardly shepherded both of my charges inside. I
grabbed a cart from inside the entrance, just so I could lean
on it and have somewhere for my crutches to sit. I scooped
up things as I passed, not really caring what I was
choosing because Jason was worryingly pale.

Only at the kids' part did I pause a little longer, and
encouraged Daisy to help me choose what she wanted,
which was everything that had pink in it from the tiny T-
shirts to the little leggings, to the slip-on sneakers. I
bundled everything in, and paid the bill without hesitation,
then headed home, Jason weighed down by bags, Daisy
walking next to me, her hand on Cap's back.

We'd gotten as far as Sean and Ash's place when I
realized that Jason wasn't walking with me. He'd stopped
at the end of the front yard, the shopping on the ground,
gripping the railing by the gate.

"Jason?" I knocked on Ash's door then encouraged
Daisy to sit on the porch. "I'm just checking on your dad,"
I explained, and pulled out the pink Nike teddy she'd
asked for. She took it from me with care and cuddled it
close and then nodded, and I headed straight back to Jason.

"Come on, Jason, let's get you inside."

He opened his eyes partially and pressed a hand to his
chest. "Promise me you'll look after Daisy," he said, his
words scratchy, breathless, and worrying.

"I'm getting you inside—"

"Promise me," he gasped, and let go of the railing to
grip my shirt. "Look after Daisy, whatever."

"I promise." I agreed without knowing what the hell
was going on. I wouldn't let anything happen to Daisy, but
that was because I wasn't only a cop, but a man who

looked out for his friends and family. He must have heard the conviction in my voice, because he let go of me, and then he swayed, not with the need to touch, but because the world was spinning in front of him, and abruptly I was buried on the ground under a heap of barely conscious Jason.

FOURTEEN

Jason

THE PAIN in my chest had worsened in the sports store, the anxiety of being outside, of watching everyone, it all tumbled and churned inside me, and I swayed against the railing, or a tree, or anything that could hold me up. I couldn't catch my breath, my vision blurring, and the earth moved. Were we having an earthquake? I needed to get to Daisy, and I needed to hold onto her and shield her from everything. But I couldn't move, someone was calling my name, and then strong arms gripped me.

"Breathe," Leo shook me a little to focus my attention, and I stared into his eyes, lost in the green of them, and listened to him talk, *in, out, in, hold, out...* the world stopped spinning, and I got a sense of where I was, on the ground half lying on Leo who was holding me firmly, and I relaxed into him. It had been so long since someone had held me, supported me, and I craved the warmth of his hold more than anything right now. It didn't occur to me that I was crushing him, but I focused on the fact that he could make things better, he could keep Daisy safe, he could hold me tight and make me believe that someone was there for me. I dropped my gaze to his lips where he was breathing with me, and I wanted to taste him. *So much need inside.* I swayed again, this time closer to him, and for a second, I could imagine the kiss. He'd be firm and comforting and sexy—everything I ever wanted.

He pushed me up, not a shove, but easing me away from him, and Sean was assisting us and helping me up some steps and into a house. Daisy clutched at my pants leg, and I wanted to hold her, but I could hardly walk, let alone carry her.

"Sit him down," Sean was saying, and then other voices joined into one long monologue in my head until I screwed my eyes shut and told them to stop. I don't think I shouted it, I don't know if I even managed to force the words out, but Sean was talking to me now, asking me when I last ate, what happened when I'd stumbled over Cap.

My head felt as if it was full of cotton wool, and I closed my eyes.

Then there was peace.

"So, this goes there, and... yep... that's right. Cap leave it alone. CAP! Quick girls, get it off him." There was giggling, Leo's voice, and a low playful growl from Cap, the kind that a dog lets out when they are having a tug of war with a toy. "Let go of Lulu, Cap!" I heard Daisy say, and she was laughing, almost as if she was happy. I blinked my eyes open to find myself propped up on a sofa.

"Daddy!" Daisy exclaimed and climbed me like a tree until she could hug me close. I ignored the pain because

Daisy was there, she was safe, laughing, and everything was okay.

"Hey," Sean said from my side, as he untangled Daisy from me and helped her to sit down with Cap. "Seems like not eating, not drinking, and then nursing severely bruised ribs along with no sleep meant you had a thing."

"A thing?" I asked because that sounded so unofficial that for a moment, I forgot Sean was a doctor.

"A panic attack of sorts, your breathing was all out of sync."

I hadn't had a panic attack since my first day in prison when the door had shut on me, and the deal I'd made to keep Rain and our child safe had collided with reality. I honestly thought I'd lost all of that shit and had become a stronger person.

Yeah right.

So what did I say now? Should I thank Sean? Instead, I pressed a hand to my aching arm then followed down to the back of my hand, where a cannula sat. I glanced around, realized I was back in Leo's place.

What happened?

"Why didn't you tell me the pain was so bad?" Sean's lips thinned, and he stared at me accusingly. I don't think that I was winning him over at all.

"It wasn't, but last night I fell on the landing…"

"Well, I put you on a drip, because you're dehydrated." Then he looked up at Leo, who was hovering. "Don't go telling anyone I have this here."

He mimed zipping his lips, and Leo nodded, then Sean turned to me.

"You should feel better soon, but we need to talk."

Fuck, that didn't sound good. Whenever someone said

to me that they needed to talk something over, it never ended well.

"What about?" I was cautious and checked past him at Daisy, who was hovering by my feet and staring at me unflinchingly. I didn't want the doc asking me all sorts of personal questions in front of Daisy, and he appeared to have had the same thought because he glanced up at Leo, who rolled his eyes and then turned to Daisy and Mia.

"Want to see Cap catch a Frisbee?" he asked, but even though Mia scampered to the door, Daisy stayed right where she was.

"Go on, Daisy, everything will be okay."

She narrowed her eyes, and God, she looked like her mom right there, and she only relaxed when I smiled at her reassuringly. I tried my best smile, but it was still a few moments before she relaxed, and after shooting Sean a glance, she followed Leo to the door and instructed Cap to follow her, although he'd been at the door at the mention of a Frisbee.

When the door shut on them, Sean moved to sit on the sofa opposite.

"Start from the beginning," he encouraged.

The beginning? No fucking way.

When I didn't say anything, Sean forged ahead. "The only thing that is stopping me from taking you to the hospital is that Leo asked me not to," he said, and then placed his hands on his knees and stared at me pointedly. "Now, tell me what hurts, what happened, in order."

Oh. He didn't mean the *real* beginning. He meant when I was hurt.

Billy had followed me from the hospital where I'd left Rain, back to the hotel room I'd taken. Daisy hid in the closet, and I confronted him, and she didn't come out because I told her to stay with her eyes shut and her hands firmly over her ears. I said I would get help.

"Your neck?" Sean prompted.

I lifted my hand, the one without the cannula, and touched my throat, which was still painful even now, despite the bruises coming out.

Sean tilted his head, eyes narrowed. "So whoever it was, tried to choke you," he summarized, "to unconsciousness? Or were they trying to kill you?"

Billy wasn't playing, demanding to know where Daisy was as he hurt me, telling me that Daisy was his, shouting at me that it was my fault Rain was in a coma. But, hurting me wasn't only about Daisy; this was just Billy killing me. I'd scrabbled hard to get away, managed to get my fingers under his hands, and flip so that he crashed into the wall. No way was Daisy watching me die in front of her.

"Jason? Tell me about your neck?" Sean asked, and I snapped back to the present.

"My arm twisted badly, I thought he was… my arm, I thought it was dislocated, but I got him off me before he could…" What the hell kind of sense would he make from my rambling?

"Okay," Sean leaned forward. "And then what happened."

The mirror by the vanity cracked, and for a second, it seemed to stay whole, hanging precariously by two screws in the flimsy wall, and then it slipped and shattered into a hundred pieces. Billy fell back onto the glass, blood there, and he grabbed the nearest section and lunged at me.

"I was cut," I said to Sean as I shuddered at the memory.

"On your belly, and your right leg? Your neck again."

He lost his temper when I lied and told him Daisy wasn't here, tried to slash me open, said he'd make me bleed to death. All I could think was that I'd told Daisy to shut her eyes and cover her ears and hoped she wouldn't see any of this. I shoved Billy back, and he hit his head, falling still for long enough that I could fetch Daisy from her hiding place, cover her eyes with my jacket, and grab her bag. And we ran past the Fed who was supposed to be protecting us, some kid called Ed, unconscious in a heap. I'd checked the press, but there was nothing about a murder in a hotel, so I assumed Billy was still alive. No one tried to find me and arrest me. Billy would have vanished as quickly as he'd arrived to find me.

"But we got away," I said, and met his gaze.

"Would you consider coming in anonymously for an X-ray—"

"No," I snapped, my heart beating frantically. "You said I'm dehydrated. That's all." I threw back his own words at him, and he shook his head. "I don't have symptoms of concussion, and my ribs don't hurt now," I blurted. There was no way I was allowing anything to take me away to a hospital.

"The muscle relaxants are—"

"Does someone still want to hurt you?" Leo interrupted, and I startled and looked up at him. How long had he been standing there? Why hadn't Sean told me?

"Where's Daisy?" Panic gripped me, and I stood so fast that I had a head rush.

It was Leo who grabbed and steadied me. "She's okay; she's right there with Asher." He pointed at the back door, and I saw Daisy sitting cross-legged with her back to me, with the man Sean was married to, fussing over Cap who was rolling around on the grass, wagging his tail. She was good with Cap, or was he good with her? Either way, they were becoming firm friends, and I relaxed a little.

"Jason?" Leo prompted again.

"Huh?" I glanced up at Leo, who was watching me closely.

"Does someone still want to hurt you?"

There was no added "What did you do?" Or anything that sounded as if he was asking me why it had happened. His tone was even, and even though I'd told myself that I wouldn't trust anyone but Eric, the way he spoke filled me with the hope that maybe I could be honest.

Not about it all, just enough so he let things lie, then Daisy and I could stay there quietly for the next few weeks.

"They would have no idea I was here," I finally answered, and he stiffened and then nodded as if he'd understood what I wasn't saying.

"This is your chance to tell us everything," Sean pressed. "Or at least to tell Leo."

"Not now." I would've done anything to keep Daisy safe, even running with her when I thought she was in danger, but I had some time because no one would put me together with Eric, who didn't even live here anymore.

"Get some rest; your ribs are bruised, and I've left some pain meds. Take them, okay? Break the cycle of pain and sleep," Sean instructed. Then to Leo, he added, "I'm on duty tonight, but I'll be back to check in on everything late tomorrow."

After he'd gone, Leo handed me tablets and water, waited with his arms crossed over his chest until I'd swallowed them, and only then did he relax. Ash and Mia had gone back next door, and Daisy had come indoors. She and Cap were involved in some complicated hedgehog story which included the poor dog wearing a cowboy hat, and inch by inch I felt my muscles relax, and the pain shifted.

My burner phone was silent, no messages, nothing saying that Austin had found Billy, or that Daisy and I were safe. The only news I had seen was an item I'd seen on the downfall of Silas Hinsley-King and how his sentencing was set. By Friday I would know how long he'd been put away for, but he didn't worry me, I was small fry, and he would never know it was me who'd shared his files with the FBI because I was good at what I did. Then Austin had to find Billy and arrest him.

And finally, I could keep Daisy safe.

FIFTEEN

Leo
———

THE REST of the day was one awkward moment after another, and not exactly how I'd planned to spend it.

No, you were planning to be in your lonely house, with your dog, and sulk with your broken leg and an entire season of some Netflix show. Get over it.

I had one eye on a dozing Jason, another on Daisy who was one moment playing quietly, and another running around the house with Cap like a mad thing. I checked in with Bella, but she was out all day up in LA, and that left me torn between just heading over to the station to check Jason out myself or waking him up and demanding he tell me what or who he was hiding from.

I lost count of the number of times I felt I had to check there was no Amber alert on a little girl or a BOLO out on anyone who could be Jason. I tried *Homeland*, and lost the plot two minutes in, began to read my book, then got distracted by organizing a food delivery, not knowing how long the two of them would be there.

Cap sidled up to me and pressed himself against my

leg, staring up at me with imploring eyes, as if he was confused about why we hadn't gone for our regular run. I scratched behind his ears with one hand, holding my mug in the other and tended to agree with him that this was one weird-ass situation. I didn't need to worry about leaving the house for work, not until after Christmas, at least, given I'd been told to add my enormous amount of vacation owed to my recovery time. But, at what point did I feel I could stop watching Jason and Daisy? Who the hell was Jason really? Ex-con? Father? Attractive guy, who'd lost all his confidence and replaced it with fear? What was he involved in right now that meant he needed to stay here and for no one to know?

My phone vibrated, and I picked it up immediately, desperate to connect to someone outside of the house, not even hesitating when I saw it was Mama, who'd be able to see right through me if I let down my defenses.

"Hi," I said and listened to a stream of Italian I had no hope of unraveling correctly. I'd tried to learn the language, but real Italian wasn't what Mama stuck to, tending to mix Italian and New York English at random times, and what she said only seemed to make sense to her.

"... and that was it, gone," she ended with a dramatic sigh, and I had clearly missed something, but woe betides anyone admits they hadn't been listening.

"Oh no," I said because it seemed appropriate. "Can I do anything to help?"

She huffed. "Unless you know how to fix a furnace, then no."

"Uhm, not really, sorry."

"So you bring someone to Thanksgiving?" she asked, or stated, you could never tell with Mama.

I guess I was because I couldn't leave Jason and Daisy in the house on their own in case they left when I wasn't there. But why did that even matter to me? Because if they left, then they weren't my concern anymore. Yeah, right. It wasn't only the cop in me that was all protective; it was a nagging thought that I could be the one to keep Jason and Daisy safe and that somehow they might need me. I considered asking Sean to come and sit over here, but why? To keep them from leaving? Or to keep them safe? My head spun with the indecision, but when it came to Thanksgiving, in the end, there was none for it.

"Of course I'll be there, Mama, same as usual." I said the same thing every time she reminded me, but today I had one thing to add. "I could be bringing someone with me."

"A girlfriend? A boyfriend? Papa!" she called to my dad before I could stop her. "Leo is bringing someone to Thanksgiving dinner! So is it a boy or a girl? Or neither? Or both? A 'they' maybe? I mean, I don't know these days, but Sheila, you remember her? At the grocery store, she said her friend's cousin is—"

"Mama, *his* name is Jason, you know him, he was the one who saved Eric in the fire. He and his daughter, Daisy, are staying here for a few days."

"A hero! So is he now *friend* also?" She latched onto that one word, and what could I tell her? He wasn't that kind of *friend*, but what was the point in explaining?

"Yes, Mama."

"Bring then, your new man, bring everyone," she said with a near squeal that I swear was so high pitched that Cap would've heard even if he'd been in the garden. "I see you next Thursday, so exciting. Love you so much sweetheart."

"Love you, too, Mama," I said even as she cut the call. Great. The last time Mama had decided to invite one of my partners to dinner, one hell of a long time ago, it had only been once, and she'd scared the life out of him, so much so that we broke up that week. I'm not sure that he'd been able to handle the way my Mama had been organizing our wedding on our third date.

"Could I get something for Daisy?" Jason asked from the door. He didn't seem as pale as before, and he'd had another shower, his hair was damp and still caught up in Mama's call, for a moment, I blinked up at him.

"Huh?" I asked, unable to channel any rational part of my brain.

"She said she's hungry, and I know we don't have... just a cookie or something."

I glanced at the clock, saw it was way past when I would do lunch, and nodded. "I'll make lunch. Does Daisy have any allergies?"

He opened his mouth, then shut it again, clearly unable to decide what to say.

"I don't know," he finally offered, "but I don't think so." He was so confused, and I fought the impulse to pull him close and tell him everything was going to be okay even if I had to lie.

"So you haven't spent a lot of time with Daisy then?"

He looked incredulous. "Did you forget I was in prison?"

"What about visits?"

"No."

"I get that, sometimes it's hardest on the kids, and she

was just a baby." I thought about that for a moment. Daisy was coming up to four, right? Jason had been inside nearly that long. "Did you know that your... partner... was pregnant?" I asked abruptly, and he blinked up at me. "I mean, did she tell you?"

"She told me," he hedged, but stared down at the counter. There was more to that story, I was sure, but I don't think he was adding anything himself.

I opened the fridge and peered in, eggs, bacon, milk, mushrooms, tomatoes. "You think Daisy likes omelets? Or scrambled eggs?"

"Eggs, I guess," he said, and then seemed to pull himself together. "Eggs are good, I've seen her eat eggs, and toast, and peanut butter." He snapped his fingers. "She's not allergic to peanuts then."

Limping around the kitchen with purpose felt good, and when Daisy cleared her plate of eggs and wheat toast, I felt as proud of my cooking skills as when I'd managed to get Mia to eat an entire bowl of chicken and rice. She'd refused it from Sean, Asher, and Eric, but not from her Uncle Fido. Nope, for me, she'd cleared her plate, and I wasn't sure if it was because I was the only one who didn't make airplane noises or because she'd already fought the others, and her resistance had been worn down. I liked to think it was my winning personality.

"You're smiling," Daisy observed, and pointed her fork at me.

I snapped back to the table and held my smile. "There's a lot to smile about."

She was confused. "Like what?"

"Daisy, you can't ask that," Jason interjected, but I waved him off.

"It's a sunny day, Cap likes to go for swims in the pool, and I was just thinking about the pool."

"I wanna go," Daisy said decisively.

Which is how we found ourselves by the pool. It was surrounded by a fence now since Mia was often over, and the locked gate meant Daisy wouldn't wander into the area and fall into the water. Something that I'd worried about, and which was underlined by the fact that she'd somehow gotten downstairs before us that time. I'd need to up the security even more, notably since Jason still spent a lot of time checking around himself, out of windows. I don't know who he expected to come here, but I wasn't taking chances.

"I didn't know she liked water," he murmured as she splashed about in the shallow end in her T-shirt and shorts, covered in sun cream from head to toe. "I know she loves the bath, but maybe I was wrong about Rain, maybe she actually…"

"What?"

"Never mind."

And there ended that small glimpse into the Jason-psyche. Daisy wasn't keen on going any deeper, and Cap was happy to stay with her instead of indulging in his love for swimming. Jason watched from the side, his bare legs dangling in the pool, never taking his eyes off Daisy, and I regretted the fact I couldn't get in the water. Still, I got involved in a playful tug of war over a Frisbee and decided that I could help out with Daisy's request for splashing Jason.

After all, the guy was just sitting there, looking hot and worried.

Of course, Daisy's splashing was hardly felt, but I'd

grown up as part of a noisy family of four and then had lived with Eric and Sean, and I knew exactly how to scoop my hands, along with the Frisbee to drench Jason. Daisy laughed, Cap barked, and Jason wiped the water from his face and smiled.

Was it possible that he would get into the pool, and for a few moments, the shadows in his eyes would go away?

"You wait until you get out, Daisy-May," he teased with a fake growl, and Daisy laughed more, hiding behind Cap.

"Cap will save me!" she shouted, and I couldn't help smiling at the interaction. I just *really* wished that Jason would have gotten in the pool with her.

We trooped back into the house, trailing wet towels, stopping only to dry anything off Daisy that the sun hadn't dealt with. The rest of the day was more of the same, Jason dozing, Daisy in his arms clutching a red dragon, and playing a game with exploding sneezing fluff balls that I'd found on my iPad.

"We can leave whenever you want us to," he said to me when we sat down for dinner.

"You'll stay where I can see you, right here in this house until Eric is home. He'd want me to let you stay, and he'd want to see you." Maybe I came over as strident, but he did at least nod.

His fingers moved restlessly against the table, tapping out the rhythm to some unknown song in his head. I think maybe it was both a nervous reaction and one that comforted him.

"We'll see what happens."

I let out a noisy sigh, and poked at my phone with feeling, scrolling through a news app, then weather, and then back to the news, not seeing any of it, and rolling everything around in my head.

Jason was lost in thought and staring into space.

Both of us, it seemed, were here waiting for Eric.

We ate in silence, Daisy drooping a little, and then abruptly, Jason said the two of them were going to bed, and my day was over. Cap and I went for a limp-walk around the block, not too far, and always keeping the house in sight. I was annoyed at the pain in my leg, and at myself for caring that Jason and Daisy might run.

I shouldn't care. Right?

But I did.

SIXTEEN

Jason
_____

EVEN THOUGH THIS was the most comfortable bed, I'd slept in since I could remember, sleep was a long time coming again, filled with restless dreams. I would wake myself up, tapping some unknown rhythm on the covers, fleeting remnants of my darkest thoughts chasing me into the room. In some of them, I was back home with my family. In others, I was back in that hotel room, unable to run and being strangled by Billy. I wished my brain could've fixated itself on one thing and one thing only. Daisy went to sleep fast, clutching her dragon, and didn't need me to worry about her, but I watched her for the longest time every single time I woke up.

In the pool today, with Cap, she'd been so... happy. I didn't know what to make of it, or whether I should take it for what it was, or that trauma had pushed what was happening to the back of her mind. She would need counseling, and I was determined to get it for her as soon as we stopped running and ended up in Vermont or wherever we put down roots.

I lost count of the number of times I'd woken up, checked on Daisy in a panic, and then attempted to get back to sleep. I was restless, thirsty, pissed off at myself, and needed to get out of this room. The door to Leo's room was shut, and I carefully picked my way over Cap, who woke up and followed me downstairs, the *click-clacking* of his paws a reassuring sound in the dark. Getting to the kitchen without stubbing my toes was one thing, but finding a mug in the dark was another, so I flicked on the stove light, filled a cup with water, and sat at the table.

"Hey." I wasn't surprised when Leo joined me, yawning and heading straight to the fridge to haul out a carton of milk, pouring some into a mug before slipping into the seat facing me, scrubbing his face with his hands before yawning again. "Can't sleep?" I nodded, and he sighed. "The bed, Daisy, your injuries, or your dreams?"

"Huh?"

"What's keeping you awake? Is it the bed? Are you worrying about Daisy? Are you in pain? Or is it dreams?"

"All of the above," I said and sipped my water, the coolness of it soothing my aching throat. I seemed to recall that Sean said that pain would get better with time, but right now, it felt as if I was swallowing past cut glass, and it sucked.

"Do you want to talk?" Leo asked.

Yes, I wanted to share everything, tell him about Billy, how much I just wanted to leave with Daisy, and then explain how most of my nightmares ended with me and Daisy dying.

"No."

He hummed under his breath and then heaved himself up to go to the counter and pull out several plastic containers. I couldn't help but stare at the strip of skin where his T-shirt pulled up from his shorts. I tried not to look, but the memories of our first kiss, and the fact he was *right there* was enough to make me unable to take my gaze off him.

He'd said he shouldn't have kissed me, hell if I could recall properly it was just his way of shutting me up at the time. All he'd done was offer to help, but if he checked too far into why I'd been in jail, then he might find out about Rain, and then everything would go to hell.

What would it be like to kiss Leo for real? He'd been demanding, cutting me off as I'd explained that I wanted him to back the fuck off. He'd tasted of fresh coffee and mint, and I could remember the taste of him even now.

"Midnight feast." He turned and faced me, and caught me staring again. I lowered my gaze, but not before I'd seen a flare of awareness in his expression. He knew I'd been watching him, but at least he didn't know what was going through my head.

From under my lashes, I saw him make a small pile of things, right between us, of stuff he'd found in the cabinet. "It's what we had left after Halloween, and with Eric not here, it doesn't get eaten. Help yourself."

I glanced up at him to see if he was messing with me, but he waved at the candy and winked, so I reached for the Milk Duds, and he hummed in approval, the sound of it going straight to my cock. What kinds of noises would he make in bed?

Why the hell am I even thinking about this? I can barely fucking breathe, let alone be able to have someone fuck me into the mattress.

"Good choice." He snapped me out of my runaway thought. "Try one now."

I couldn't recall the last time I'd had one of these, and I tore apart the tiny pack's wrapper carefully and peered into it. "Is it only me, or is candy getting smaller now?"

He laughed then, a sweet sound that echoed in the quiet kitchen. "Have you maybe thought it's just us getting bigger?"

"I remember the Duds being huge."

"Maybe the real ones are, but these are the Halloween treat-sized packs, so I don't contribute to rotting kid's teeth, which was the aim of the lecture I got from Sean when he saw me hauling in full-size packs."

I felt hopeful, "Wait, you have full-size packs of Milk Duds in this house?"

He leaned back in his chair and patted his flat belly. "Ate one, took the rest into work."

It hit me as we talked that this was the first real non-fucked up exchange of words we'd had since forever, and it was nice.

"Yeah." I chewed the candy in silence. Then, with the tiny pack finished, all five of the Duds gone, and with mischief in mind, I snaked out a hand and grabbed the other little candy bar. When I looked up at him, he was grinning like an idiot, and yeah, he had a gorgeous smile.

"It's like that, is it?" He pulled the Skittles toward him, four small bags of them, then he lifted an eyebrow in challenge. This was a stupid childish game and one that made me feel lighter even in the middle of the night. Not only that, but he was smiling, and hell, I was smiling as well.

I took the Twix, which made him curse, and I fist-pumped to know I'd beaten him to his other favorite. He reached for the Twix, but I captured his hand, and for a few seconds, we wrestled over the candy, both smiling like idiots. Then he stopped playing, and I stopped holding him off, and abruptly, we'd laced fingers without even meaning to.

"Jason…" he murmured, but I couldn't answer, and I didn't want to touch him. He was sexy and rumpled, and his smile charmed the gods, and I wanted to be inside his world of fucking sunshine and rainbows so much that it was dangerous. As it was, I'd need a cold shower to get my cock to settle down. We untangled our fingers, but the spark of attraction was there in the warmth of our joined touch. Then he changed the subject, attempting to lighten the tone.

"Okay then, I'm next, and if the guy whom I gave a bed to isn't going to be nice to me…" He snorted a laugh, then fished out a single Twinkie, and that left the two of us with the choice of candy corn and Sour Patch Kids. I didn't want either, but it was my turn, and I didn't want this stupid-ass game to end. If I was being polite, I'd have offered him the choice, but that wasn't the point of this game, and I decided that candy corn was the lesser of two evils, scooping all three bags of them and adding them to my pile.

Leo took the remaining items and shook his head. "Can't believe you did that to me, dude," he murmured and patted the Sour Patch Kids. "The devil's candy," he shuddered, then looked over at my pile and did this dimpled pout frown thing.

"I can swap," I said immediately, but he shook his head, and there was that devastating smile back again.

"I'm messing with you. We had a fair division of the spoils."

Neither of us ate much of what we'd piled there, but it had been funny and *fun* to get to this point. I still wasn't tired, and now I was probably going to have a sugar high and bounce off the walls.

"You want a drink?" Leo asked. "Hot chocolate?"

The night was warm, but the thought of hot chocolate sounded perfect. Anyway, I could ogle him again as he made it, and think about all the what-ifs.

What if I hadn't taken the fall for something I didn't even do?

What if I was brave enough to hold onto his hand and admit that I couldn't get him out of my head even when I was at my lowest? Even if when he kissed me, he'd been so shocked at what he'd done.

What if he saw me as something other than a bad guy who didn't deserve to be kissed?

We drank in silence, and I was beginning to feel tired. Almost as if I might be able to lie down and actually sleep.

"We should try and sleep," he read my mind.

I left the candy on the table and began to head upstairs, Leo on my heels. I owed him something, a thank-you for taking us in maybe, or gratitude for not asking too many questions, and I stopped on the landing next to an alert Cap, to say the words.

I turned to face Leo in the soft glow of the nightlight he'd plugged in for Daisy. It was one of two, the other one in the shape of the moon by her side of the bed. She loved it and tried to convince me that she would stare at it all night until, of course, she fell fast asleep.

Leo was right there in my space again, carefully

picking his way over Cap, his palm on the wall, watching where he stepped.

"Do you remember the kiss?" he asked me in the half-dark.

"Yes. I remember it."

He winced and then held my gaze. "I recall the argument we were having, every single word of you telling me to fuck off out of your life, stop asking questions, and then me grabbing you and kissing you to stop you shouting. I remember my regrets."

Disappointment welled inside me. For a moment, I'd thought he was going to tell me that it wasn't a mistake and that his whispered *what have I done* meant something other than implying he had a million regrets.

That kiss had haunted me for the longest time after, knocked my absent self-esteem even lower.

"Yeah, you said at the time," I said and reached for the door handle to my and Daisy's room, but he stopped me, gripping my hand and holding tight.

"I know what I said, and I'm sorry."

I tugged my hand away. "Why are you sorry? You kissed me, and you shouldn't have, you said so."

"You don't understand."

"I don't really want to," I feigned boredom, but he retook my hand, this time more gently.

"I didn't regret kissing you when I said that."

"Sounded like it to me."

"Fuck," he scrubbed at his eyes. "I swear that I didn't mean that I shouldn't have kissed you. I just meant it wasn't appropriate at that time, and I should have waited."

"That's what you say now," I tried to lighten the conversation as this was getting way too intense.

"Listen to me, Jason. I'm sorry because what I regretted most was that we didn't get to kiss again."

I turned to face him. "Huh?"

"Also, I didn't listen to you and looked into your case, anyway. There was no reason you had to go to prison, no evidence that conclusively pointed to you embezzling that money from iTech, yet you didn't fight the charge. Why?"

Jeez, that's a leading question.

"I did what I had to do for my family."

He tugged me closer, and I didn't pull back, not until he turned and pressed me against the wall, trapping me there with one hand holding mine and the other flat on the wall against my head.

"I know you did," he whispered, and then he kissed me. The touch was gentle, a whisper of a thing that barely registered, but it turned my world upside down. As we separated, I knew this was the kiss I'd promised myself, the one thing I could cross off my list. I should reject him, tell him I regretted kissing him, then go into my room and attempt to sleep. Then I could focus on the next thing I could do to start my new life with Daisy.

"Leo—"

He stopped me with a thorough, toe-curling kiss that was the sexiest thing I'd ever experienced with my clothes on. My legs turned to jelly, and I gripped his shirt as he slanted the kiss, and our tongues tangled lazily. This wasn't like the kiss in the bathrooms—that had been short, sharp, and over in a few seconds, but this was an exploration and a promise all wrapped into one.

I shrugged my hand free of his hold, and for a moment, he stopped kissing me, but I didn't want that. I laced my fingers behind his head, holding on, and even tilting my head a little to get a better angle. I didn't want just the one-sided kiss. I wanted to feel everything that I thought might be there, the connection I'd craved during my lowest times in prison, despite the fact he'd said he shouldn't have kissed me at all. He caressed my tongue with his, no aggressive thrusting, no pushing me flat against the wall, no anger, or lust, this was a gentle exploration, and I was lost.

Regret, affection, need, and despair washed over me in a flood, and grief choked in my throat. He'd promised me he would help me if I needed it, and I'd dismissed him out of hand, and now it was all too late for help. I pulled back a little, and he chased for the kiss, his eyes shut, only stopping when it was apparent I didn't want more.

"Jason?"

"You hate this, you don't want to kiss an ex-con."

"I do."

"You don't see past that."

"Jason, please—"

"I'm not who you think I am," I interrupted. "Daisy is my priority. I have a past, and you're a cop, none of this works."

"If nothing works, then why have I wanted to kiss you for so long, and why do I want to look after you? I should be digging into who hurt you, and why you're even here, yet all I'm doing is sitting on my ass when I should be doing something. *Anything.*"

His statement threw me, but I couldn't have a heart-to-heart tonight, I needed some space. I untangled my hands and stepped away, then climbed over Cap to get to my room, slipping inside and shutting the door. For a few moments, I leaned against the wood, the soft rumble of

Leo talking to Cap was all I could hear, and then there was a door shutting. He was in his room. I was in mine.

Which was precisely how it should be.

I woke every half-hour in a panic and decided that tonight, I would put something in front of the door, like the chair that came with a small desk in the corner. Then, if Daisy woke and I was asleep and she moved the seat, I would hear her. But that had been my idea at three-thirty. By four, I was worried about getting trapped in the room in a fire, which meant that between four and five I was in that anxious state I thought I'd overcome in prison.

Fuck my life.

At breakfast, I didn't want to have to use Daisy as a metaphorical shield to hide behind, but I would if I needed to. Shamelessly and without hesitation, which probably made me a bad dad, but hell, I'd had no sleep, and Leo had this way about him that made me want things I couldn't have. I had to face him after what had happened last night, and I had some words in my head to explain that acting on attraction was wrong, but the minute I stepped into the kitchen, the words fled.

Because he wasn't alone.

He already had his hands out in front of him, all innocence. "Before you say a word, this is Lillian, she's a friend of Sean's, and she's a pediatric psychiatrist. He asked her to visit in complete confidence."

I scooped Daisy up, and I don't know why I did because she'd been having a perfectly friendly morning hug with Cap, and all she did was struggle to get down. All I knew was that there was a stranger in the house and that this new person was checking me out with a considering gaze.

She had kind eyes, but ultimately she had this assessing feel about her. For a moment or two, I was caught in that middle space between feeling safe and running for the hills, and I wanted to shout at Leo that I wasn't ready for people in my and Daisy's lives. On the other hand, I was desperate for someone, *anyone I could respect*, to tell me that Daisy was going to be okay.

"I've come for breakfast," Lillian said and sipped her coffee. "That's all."

"That's not all, is it? I don't have the money to... why did you even..." Words failed me, and I looked at Leo for help. He wasn't much use, simply sitting at the table where all kinds of breakfast bits and pieces were laid out, along with coffee and orange juice.

"Let's just eat breakfast."

My head was too full, but at last I let Daisy down, who scrambled to finish her hug with Cap and then climbed up onto a stool.

"Hello, Daisy, my name is Lillian," she introduced herself, and even just that simple thing was enough to make me tense.

"Hi," Daisy said after checking with me first. What was I going to do, tell her not to say hello? Was I really going to make a scene here? This was not how I was expecting the morning after last night to go at all. This wasn't awkward discussions about why kissing was a bad idea. This was some expert in children judging my daughter. What happened if the doc thought I was wrong for her?

I helped Daisy with her pancakes, then as she was still hungry, I cut off some of my untouched bagel, and she accidentally-on-purpose dropped it to the floor where it was vacuumed up by Cap.

"No feeding the dog," I was firm, hating the sound of my voice and knowing for sure that I was fucking this up. Only Leo didn't feed Cap between meals, and I wanted to do right by the person who was giving us a bed to sleep in.

"He looks hungry," Daisy said and blinked at me in innocence. God, she could charm a monkey out of a tree.

"He's not hungry, Daisy, so no more, okay?"

She pouted, but then everything was forgotten as she sipped her juice. I was on edge waiting for the doc to start asking questions, feeling as if she and Leo were staring at me, and my head hurt. But it was Leo who came to my rescue.

"Did you sleep okay, Daisy?" he asked, and passed her some more juice when she'd finished what she had.

"Uh, huh," she bobbed her head. I nudged her with my arm. "Thank you," she added, and then grinned up at me so hard that my heart expanded with love.

I'd dreamed in prison of seeing her smile, only it hadn't been in a cop's kitchen, but in the woods behind some house I'd rented in Hill Valley, in a coat and boots, splashing in puddles, laughing, playing with fallen leaves.

I always pictured her that way, in a place of safety with me and her mom sharing childcare in whatever complicated plan we'd concocted to split our daughter's time.

"What about you?" Leo asked, and I had to pull myself out of her smile, which was impossibly hard.

"Me?"

He dimpled a grin at me, which was as bright as Daisy's. "Did you sleep okay?"

I could lie, and tell him what he wanted to hear, I was stressed and tired, and honesty was all I could find. "I didn't want to wake up alone," I said, and side-eyed Daisy, who swung her legs on the stool.

"I get that," he said.

"Leo was telling me you like the pool," Lillian stated, and Daisy nodded vigorously, her curls waving. She probably needed a haircut or something to hold her bangs from her face, sooner rather than later, and I made a mental note of that, and also to make a list of the things I needed for her. A copy of her birth certificate, immunization records, anything that helped me form a picture of my beautiful little girl before she'd come into my life. Because, unless Rain woke up, I had nothing from before I'd taken her and ran.

"I don't swim good," she murmured.

"Well," I corrected, and she wrinkled her nose.

"Well, I don't swim good," she said, and I just wanted to hug her so tight. I could've corrected her, but inside I was laughing, and I needed to hold onto that thought.

"Good enough," I said, and we bent in and touched noses.

"You had fun, though," Lillian interrupted our little ritual, and I wanted to be angry, but I mostly wanted to hear the answer.

"Lots. Can I go play now, Daddy?"

I wasn't going to make her stay just to talk to Lillian, but it seemed Lillian had other ideas anyway.

"Do you like to color? I have a hundred different crayons, all the colors of the rainbow, would you like to see them?"

Again, she glanced at me for reassurance, and I felt

like the best father in the world that she'd looked to me for guidance, and then swallowed that when it occurred to me that she didn't know who to trust. Shouldn't young kids be open and trusting of everything, isn't that why they needed responsible parents?

"Yep." She went into the living room, and I could see her from here, and Lillian started to follow her, in her hands a huge box of crayons and a book. I stopped Lillian as she passed, and she waited, staring at me with expectation. What was I going to say? Should I tell her to leave Daisy alone, demand that I be there with her, or did I trust Leo wouldn't let just anyone in the house? In the end, I said nothing, but I took my coffee and perched on the sofa watching Lillian interact with Daisy and an inquisitive Cap who tried the taste of a red crayon and spat it out in disgust. Daisy laughed so hard she was close to crying, and Cap spent at least a minute licking his lips as if that would help vanish the taste of scarlet waxiness.

Lillian went into the kitchen after a while, and I followed her after checking that Daisy was okay with Bedge-Hog and Lulu, along with the myriad other hedgehog people that she'd grown confident enough to play with.

By the time I reached the kitchen, I guessed she and Leo had completed the serious discussion about what happened next, so I went from zero to sixty in seconds.

I closed the door to the front room, "She's staying with me." I was leaving nothing open for discussion.

"Of course she is," Lillian said, and frowned, "I'm not here to take Daisy anywhere, I'm here to help, to see if there is anything she needs, anything repressed, any harm, or abuse, from her life before you took her from it."

All the blood rushed from my head, and I sat heavily on the nearest stool. "Abuse, you think that…"

"I've only done an initial assessment, but she seems to be a happy child, confused, nervous, maybe a bit too anxious, but she is where she needs to be right now, with her father."

"But…"

"For what it's worth, I don't see her hiding anything, although she did mention she had a secret about knowing someone called Daddy-B, and that I wasn't allowed to tell anyone. She even covered over the dog's ears, so it must be something you asked her to do. Keep that secret, I mean."

"Only because… shit… did I fuck that up?"

Lillian shook her head, then extended a hand, which I shook. "I'd like to come back every so often, maybe every other day, just to help her talk through anything that is causing her concern. Do you know much about her life with her mom?"

That switched direction fast. She'd slipped in coming out to visit way too easy, and then swapped to talking about Rain? Shoulders back, I tilted my chin.

"First off, I don't have money for your kind of help, and second, she's going to be happy with me, and we'll sort through the situation with her mom properly."

I'm scared to think what Rain was like, but me and Daisy have to do this alone.

She nodded, then counted off on her finger. "First, this is repaying a favor to Sean, so there is no cost, and second, for what it's worth, she mentioned her mom was sad but didn't elaborate."

"Then we understand each other," I said, with defiance in my tone.

She smiled at me and pressed a hand to my arm. "I'll be back, no charge, and hey, keep up the good work, Dad."

Leo showed her out then limped back toward me, and in a smooth move that he managed despite the cast, he pulled me close and kissed me. I was too stunned to move, and when I did back off, I eyed him with suspicion.

"What the hell?"

"That means we don't have to talk about anything awkward from last night and can focus on this kiss instead."

I shoved him a little, and he bounced back on the nearest cabinet. "What? I get approval from Lillian, and suddenly it's okay for the holier-than-thou cop to kiss me?" Even as I spoke, I knew I was as an asshole, and turning everything onto him was a defense mechanism.

He chuckled low in his throat. "There's nothing holy about what I want to do to you, and anyway, it was *me* who kissed *you* last night, remember? He looked past me as the front room door opened, and Daisy came barreling in with Cap, "Also, *Jason,* gut instinct? I happen to think Daisy is lucky to have you as a dad."

SEVENTEEN

Leo

———

THE REST of the day was molasses-slow, and I knew I was
the one to blame for it. I'd not only kissed the man I was
supposed to be looking out for, so many times I'd lost
count, but I'd also told him that I thought he was a good
dad. I needed to talk about this insane simmering attraction
with someone. Anyone. Sean would talk me off the edge,
either of my brothers would laugh along with me, and they
would make me see that this crazy attraction could be
handled okay. As for my sister, well, all Lorna wanted was
for me to have a happy ending somewhere in my life, but
then she was all hearts and roses with her new boyfriend.

Eric would listen and then tease me out of my funk, but
he was up in the hills, possibly fighting the fire, maybe
bunking down in the worst of places.

Maybe I should make something of this attraction I had
to Jason, because I really felt like he could be… something
special to me. Real.

My last relationship had been with another cop, Lisa
from Narcotics, the one before that with Liam who'd

transferred to New York and before that, Luke who'd decamped to the FBI. My track record with dating fellow cops whose names started with 'L' was atrocious, and I needed to look outside of the limited dating pool. I'd even fooled myself I could love them, but none of the relationships had ever worked long-term.

According to Mama, being bisexual meant I had more options than most, but that wasn't right. I was picky, and not one single person had caught my attention. Not where I fell in love, or even lust, and never the same way as I'd seen for my friends, Sean and Eric. They were happy, and I didn't envy them that contentment; I was just lonely, and I'd concluded that this was what must have been driving my need to kiss Jason.

I rolled over in bed, moved again, took some low-grade pain pills for my leg, got restless, anxious, and then when I eventually did fall asleep, I was chased by dreams that became nightmares. Memories of childhood coalesced into images mixed in with Jason and Daisy until I woke, sweating, cursing my brain, and finally giving up and heading for the shower. I'd managed about five hours, but Cap was nowhere to be seen on the landing, and I was still down before Jason, not Daisy though, who was awake and standing by the dolls' house, with her hand on Cap.

"Morning, Daisy," I said quietly so as not to make her jump, but loud enough to startle her a little. I can't believe that I didn't hear her come downstairs; what kind of cop am I?

"Hello," she said and turned to look at me, somehow managing to ease herself behind Cap, so he was between us. I hated that she didn't trust me, but there again, at one time I had shoved her dad into a wall.

"Did you want pancakes?" I asked, hoping that would get me a smile.

"Not every day, silly," she told me, and I guess she was right, we shouldn't have pancakes every day, so I had to think on my feet.

"I have cereal, or yogurt and fruit?" I limped away from her into the kitchen, using the wall to balance myself and then proceeded to pull out every single type of cereal I'd had delivered, along with apples, bananas, bagels, cream cheese, milk, and tubs of different-flavored yogurts. I then busied myself with coffee, hearing the *click* of Cap's paws on the wood before Daisy's whispered reassurance that he'd have breakfast soon.

"Would you like to measure out Cap's kibble?" I asked as she clambered onto the stool. When Mia had first come into our lives, Sean, Eric, and I had bought new seats with backs, so that Mia didn't climb up and then fall off. Mia wasn't old enough yet to get up there, and the system hadn't been tried. So I hurried with the kibble and the measuring cup, nearly slid on my ass twice, because I'd left my crutch propped up by the stove, and at last, I was able to help Daisy count out what Cap needed to eat.

"Can I give him chippy cookies?" she asked me as she picked pieces of kibble up and placed them into the cup. I *think* by chippy she meant chocolate chip, but who knew? I decided to go with that for now.

"Chocolate is poisonous for dogs," I explained and patted Cap's head where he waited, hopping from paw to paw. "Also, he'd get to be a very fat dog if all we fed him was cookies." Cap would eat anything he could get his paws on. He'd had a loaf of bread from on top of the microwave, although how he'd gotten up that high I had no idea, an entire coffee cake from the counter, and once he'd worked his way through an entire carton of fudge, wrappers and all, which I'd then been cleaning up for weeks. Well, apart from the week I was at work, and then it had been Eric's job to clean up after him, and boy did he bitch about that.

Something I found *hilariously* funny to this day.

"Do you want to hear a funny story?" I asked, waiting for her nod. "One morning, I came down, and Cap had the lid of the trash can around his neck, where he'd pushed his way inside to get at pizza and then got his head stuck." She glanced up at me, and I wanted to make her smile. I made the shape of a swing trash can lid around my face and made googly eyes, rewarded when she giggled.

"Silly Cap," she said, and at his name, he jumped up and put his paws on the stool next to her, his tail wagging. "Silly," she said again and hugged his head. He didn't move a muscle, just kept wagging his tail, and grinning a doggy smile at me. Good boy.

On a typical day, I would have fed him after me, something I'd read in the puppy books when I'd first gotten him, but this was a special occasion. With his breakfast measured out, Daisy helped me to put it on the floor, filled his water bowl, and then we stepped back to watch him chase his kibble around this complicated spiral dog bowl. Getting each piece was a game and took him a while when he used to inhale the entire dish in a couple of gulps. It was fun to watch him, so intent on getting every last piece, and then it was our turn to eat.

She chose Lucky Charms, I went straight for my favorite Cookie Crisps, swirling them in the milk, and then eating them as slowly as Daisy did. I didn't want to finish first and made a big show of emptying my bowl at the same time as she did, and then all done, I cleared up, which she watched from her stool.

"What will Daddy eat?" she asked when I shut the dishwasher door.

"Anything he wants."

"He could eat chippy cookies," she said in all seriousness.

"He could."

There was the noise like the thundering of elephants down the stairs, and I assumed that Jason had woken up to find Daisy missing.

"Hey," Jason was breathless as he came into the kitchen, crossing to Daisy, pressing a kiss to her head and nodding to me.

Daisy pointed at me. "He said you could eat all the chippy cookies for breakfast," she told her bemused father, who pulled her into a sideways hug and gave her another kiss on her disheveled blonde curls.

"For real?" he teased. "But then what would you have with your milk later?"

"Kibble," she said and opened up her palm where one tiny dog kibble sat. I didn't move fast enough, Jason wasn't expecting it so did nothing, and we both watched in horror as she put the kibble in her mouth and crunched it down. She wrinkled her nose as she swallowed, and then looked up at her dad. "I don't like kibble," she said, and it took Jason a few seconds to fully comprehend what had just happened.

"My bad," I said, and gestured at the open bag of dog kibble, "We were feeding Cap." As excuses went, it was pretty lame, and for a moment I thought Jason was going to lose his shit, and then all his worries and concerns slipped away in an instant, and he grinned over her head at me, and it was the singularly most perfect smile I'd ever seen. He was laughing at what had just happened, and if not laughing, then at least he'd found it funny, and there was sunshine in his smile. I couldn't hold his gaze for too long, because I knew I was smiling back like an idiot.

It was Cap who broke the silence, barking at the back door, where I saw Gina's tuxedo cat walking casually past the window.

"That's Felix," I told Daisy, and she clambered down, going over to Cap and placing her hands on the window staring at the cat. "I found her already downstairs, but I'm really sorry about the kibble thing," I apologized, and he shook his head.

"She was smiling, and she talked to you, it's all good."

And that started a quiet day, when Daisy paddled in the pool with Cap, both of us watching, went to the park with the two of us and Cap, played hedgehog tea parties with Cap, and then fell asleep on the sofa curled up on Jason just after lunch.

While Jason was dozing I took the time to examine the visible bruises. He was wearing a T-shirt we'd bought at the sports store, a pale blue one that was a little large for him, and shorts in a bright purple that Sean had left behind when he'd moved out. He looked so peaceful sitting in the corner, his legs up and straight, holding Daisy close. What would it be like to have this for real? Someone on the sofa, with our child on their chest, the same as Sean and Asher had? Or having teenagers at school with hugs for anyone, like Eric and Brady did?

I made chicken parmesan for dinner, or at least I

opened the container, not up to cooking from scratch because my leg was aching by the end of the day. I knew I was doing too much, and Sean would be pissed at me, but I wanted to look after my guests, and damn it, I wanted to push through the barriers that kept me at home.

The call from Bella came through when we were eating, and I silenced it, but as soon as Jason took Daisy upstairs for her bath, I called her back.

She answered on the third ring, and mumbled hello, sounding as if she had a mouthful of food, and I heard Lewis in the background asking her who it was. Her poor husband was one of the good guys, a Fed, he knew the score when it came to my and Bella's partnership, and friendship, but I didn't want to interrupt what could have been a romantic evening together.

"Tell Lewis sorry, and that I can call again," I said immediately.

She was silent for a bit, I heard some background noise, and the sound of a door closing. "It's all good, he said he didn't think this could wait and I tend to agree, but Leo, this is all off the record and goes no further, okay?"

That sounded ominous as if she was about to impart the worst kind of news to me.

"What did you find out?"

"It's the oddest thing, but I genuinely think the FBI is involved in this somehow, before you ask, this is just a mix of intuition, a lot of walls, U-turns and redacted shit. I'm not sure you're going to like this at all."

"Okay?" What could she tell me? That whatever she'd found out was so bad that I'd broken a million laws just by having Jason and Daisy here? Not that she even knew who was living with me.

"You've seen the news, right? About Silas Hinsley-King?"

"Who hasn't?" Hinsley-King, multi-millionaire, bought his way to legitimacy, money laundering, tax evasion, human trafficking, and his whole house of cards had just fallen. He'd been arrested and pleaded guilty and was awaiting sentencing. It was a name that had haunted my father when he was a cop, and he still followed the story religiously even though he'd been retired five years.

What I knew about the man was enough to have me more than concerned. He'd never spent time behind bars, mostly because he'd bought his way out of anything thrown at him, and lived a quiet life in the Los Angeles hills. Still, it wasn't because he was an active case that I knew him, it was because my dad had been part of a task force back in the eighties that had tried to take the corrupt Hinsley-King world down.

The man had been a thorn in my dad's side, but he'd been an even greater thorn in the side of the FBI who'd lost every time they'd gone up against him. The man was slippery, and the money he'd made with crime had bought him a cloak of respectability that he pulled around himself. He'd paid off so many people he'd become untouchable, but when Dad retired, it didn't mean I hadn't kept my ears open for any mention of the name in case one day I could be part of a team that arrested Hinsley-King and make my dad one happy man. Well, he'd been arrested when a ton of secret files had flooded the internet, exposing criminal activity at such a high level that not even his high priced lawyers could get him off.

I just never expected to hear the name in any connection to Jason.

He'd moved operations from San Diego to L.A., but that didn't mean that Papa Byrne didn't remember everything or wish he'd been able to get justice for the crimes he'd seen committed by the men around Hinsley-King.

"The name you gave me, Daisy, if she's nearly four, birthday twenty-third December, blue eyes, blonde, presumed to be with her father currently, it all fits."

"Fits what?"

"Daisy is Hinsley-King's granddaughter, her mom, Rainbow-Star Murray, also known simply as Rain, is in a coma in Mercy after an overdose. Not that the blood connection between Rain and Hinsley-King is obvious unless you dig deep; she was cut out of his life at sixteen or so, and changed her last name. I had to dig way back, and she was on a watch list but disappeared. I don't know how Hinsley-King did it, but she's been erased from anything connecting them post-sixteen. It's like she died, only clearly she didn't."

"Fuck."

"Also, we have an unknown on the birth certificate for Daisy's father's name. The only real name I can connect to both Daisy and Rainbow, and this was only because I pulled in a shit ton of sexual favors with Lewis," she paused, and I heard Lewis snort. "The name I have is William Forstern, AKA Billy, a record, drug possession and supply, bit of a low life on all accounts, out of Hill Valley, Vermont."

"What is this man's connection to Daisy?" *And Jason.*

"All I can tell you is that there was a situation with Billy and an FBI agent whom he injured. Billy is in the wind; the agent is in the hospital with a skull fracture. It crossed Lewis' desk, and this is him putting two and two together, nothing more."

I waited a moment to take all of that in, and then worded my next question very carefully.

"And what about Jason? What is his connection to Billy?"

"I wish I could help you there, but the amount of redaction on some of the news is out of hand."

"Thank you, Bella, and if you find out anything else—"

"I'll pass it on if I can," she finished for me.

We exchanged goodbyes, I ended the call, and for a moment I sat still and considered what I'd just been told.

"You couldn't leave it alone, could you," Jason said from behind me, and I didn't even startle or whirl around to face him, part of me understood the inevitability of him being right behind me as I'd talked.

Cautiously, I twisted on the stool and considered his expression. He didn't look any shade of angry—if anything, he was resigned. I could apologize for doing my job, I could get angry and demand that he understand why I had to know, or I could stay quiet, but none of those options fitted.

"Who is Billy to you?" but even as I asked, the answer hit me. "Daddy-B? That's who Daisy means, the one who hurt her." I got up from the stool and wobbled on one foot, the urge to do something like a fire in my blood. "And you? Was he the one who tried to hurt you?"

"Not just hurt me. Kill me," Jason said without hesitation. "He found out where I was after I took Daisy from the hospital. I thought she was safe and away with Rain, but no, Rain had called Billy for one last hit, overdosed, ended up in the hospital, and he was there, at the hospital, must have seen me leaving. I was in a hotel suite, the Feds put me there and left someone with me to keep an eye on me until they could figure out if they had everything they needed..." He stopped then, and closed his eyes briefly, before pressing his fingers to his temples. "I made a deal, a new life for Rain and Daisy, and one for me. It was a mess."

There was so much in that confession that I had a hard time unraveling the facts, but there were two things that jumped out at me. Rain and Daisy were going to have a separate life from Jason, and Billy had tried to kill Jason.

"Was Daisy in the room—?"

"I heard Ed shout a warning—he was the FBI guy outside the door. I made her go inside the closet, then I tried to stop Billy getting in, but he's a big guy." He huffed then as if this was a story he was telling and not something so personal it had to hurt. "She didn't see anything," he added with relief, then touched the wound on his neck. "The mirror," he murmured, and I recalled what he'd told Sean about being choked and cut, and my entire being was consumed with anger and a need to hurt someone badly. Then he shook his head, clearing the thoughts he'd become lost on. "He said he was coming for Daisy, said he'd been Daisy's daddy for a year, and that if he had her, then he'd have Rain's money." He snorted, "She didn't have any money. Silas cut her off when she was fifteen, the first time he found her with drugs."

We sat at the counter, and I steeled myself for this story, wanting to touch Jason and reassure him.

"What happened?"

"I knocked him down, he was dazed, and I took Daisy

and ran. We traveled around for a while, kind of aimlessly, but I was injured, and Daisy was upset, and it was just a matter of time before I was picked up by a cop." He gestured at me, and I nodded. If I'd seen an injured man and an upset child, I would have asked questions, and he'd have been lucky to get away with not being taken in. "I didn't know who to trust, and then I remembered Eric said he'd help me any time I needed him, and that was the only thing I had to cling to. I had to get Daisy somewhere safe." He was fierce, leaning forward in the chair, his blue eyes fixed on me, and I guess he was daring me to tell him he'd been wrong.

"She is safe here," I reassured him, "with the security we have on this house, no one gets in if we don't want them to, we'll be careful until they pick up Billy."

"Okay."

"You should have told me yourself."

"I didn't know who to trust."

"You can trust me."

He looked at me with a steady fixed gaze. "I want to."

Then, I was equally as fierce and added my last word to this conversation. "I promise you I won't let anything happen to Daisy."

EIGHTEEN

Jason

I PROMISE you I won't let anything happen to Daisy.

I believed him. Even with his bum leg, I believed he would put Daisy above everything else, but maybe in a couple of days, when I felt better, it would be time for me to move on. Billy wasn't the brightest bulb on the porch, but he was intensely focused on one thing, getting me out of the way, and using Daisy to get money.

It had always been about money, and he'd find Daisy and me even in the suburbs of San Diego County with its three million-plus residents.

"Thank you."

I thought maybe that was going to be the end of this conversation, but it seemed that Leo had other ideas.

"How did you meet Rain?"

I wasn't ready to go that far, the things that had happened between Rain and me were too much to get out in the open, because it led to a shit ton of secrets, and I shook my head. "Not now," I murmured.

"But soon," Leo insisted, and then went back to

clearing up the kitchen counters. I loaded the dishwasher and washed the pan, and then there was nothing left to do except wonder what happened next. After all, last night, he'd kissed me, and today he'd been nothing but concerned, and even though the phone call had thrown information out that he wanted to challenge, we'd handled it like grown-ups.

Daisy had fallen asleep on the sofa, her hand in Cap's fur where he lay on the floor next to her. He looked at us with a sigh of doggy contentment, if that was even a thing. I covered her in a blanket and untangled her hand from him, but all he did was jump up on the sofa and curl up in the corner with his head right by her.

"That's love if I ever saw it," Leo commented and scratched Cap's furry head.

"He's a good dog. Have you had him since he was a puppy?"

Leo nodded and crouched down to press a kiss to Cap's nose. "Found him on a call, he was one of three puppies that had been put in a sack, really tiny they were, too young to be taken from their mama, but they weren't wanted, it was as if the people who'd had the care of them just saw them as garbage."

"Tell me this has a happy ending for all of them."

He smiled up at me. "Yeah, between us all, me, Eric, Sean, we hand-reared all three, this was about six years ago, and we found homes for Loki and Panther, but kept Cap because he was just... our dog by then, or mostly mine at least."

"So I'm following the trend and guess Cap is short for Captain America, right?"

"Yeah."

"I feel sorry for the one saddled with a cat's name," I realized I'd just made a joke, which could go one of two ways. I could make Leo smile, or he could get antsy with me.

"That was all on Sean. He's an idiot."

His phone vibrated, and he went back into the kitchen to talk, checking caller ID and smiling in that way I knew it was a friend, or maybe family.

"Hi, Brady," he put the phone on loudspeaker, crutched over to the cabinets and pulled down a box, nearly overbalancing, so much so, that I helped him steady himself, which put me super close and aware of him just being there.

"Just heard from Eric," Brady began, "he should be home tomorrow, day after at the latest."

"That's good news," Leo said, but he didn't move from where we stood next to each other, both holding onto the plastic container.

"I told him about Jason, and he said he'll get over as soon as he can."

I wondered how Brady had explained everything to his partner, but couldn't dwell on what other people thought of me. Otherwise, I'd worry myself to death.

They ended the call with a quick conversation about a nephew's tennis tournament, which Leo promised to attend, and then it was just him, me, and a stupid box on a counter. I should lean in because it was my turn to kiss him, right? After all, he'd been the one to put himself out there for me, and I should take a chance that this was what he wanted. But I waited so long, mired in indecision that he stepped away and broke our weird little face-off, taking the container with him.

"Chocolate?" he asked as he flipped the lid and exposed an entire collection of all kinds of hot chocolate flavorings. "You can choose."

He pulled milk from the refrigerator, chocolate from a stash in a tall cupboard, and heated the liquid on the stove, whistling low as he melted chocolate and added cream.

While he did that, I examined everything on offer, and finally decided on orange, which he took from me and added to the saucepan.

"Did you want orange as well?" I asked, a little confused as to why he just took what I gave him. I assumed he'd split the drink into two mugs and make his choice.

"As far as I'm concerned, there is nothing in there I wouldn't have in my hot chocolate, so it didn't matter what you chose. Although I'm pretty sick of the pumpkin one after the amount I drank over Halloween," he added, with a wry smile. Everything here was so damn normal, as if we just a couple of typical friends enjoying a hot chocolate, and when he suggested we carry them outside, I could go with that. He left the door open so we could see and speak to Daisy if she woke up and pulled across the thin screen, then settled at a table on a patio just outside.

We sat next to each other in cushioned chairs, and I sipped the best hot chocolate I'd ever tasted.

"When do you think Eric will get here?" I asked and tilted my head up to the stars in the clear skies of a November night.

"As soon as he can," Leo reassured me.

I wonder what he'll say. Would he offer Daisy and me a room to stay in? He said he'd do anything for me, but it had been his best friend who'd stepped up.

Even after he'd kissed me, then regretted it.

"Daisy loves Cap," I began, with thoughts of moving this discussion onto the fact that I felt it was a good place for Daisy here and that I didn't want to go, however uncomfortably challenging him kissing me was.

"Yeah, she does, and Cap loves her. Look, I know this might be awkward, and I'll get it if you don't agree, but even if Eric offers you space, it's probably best you stay here. His and Brady's place isn't huge, and they have the kids there. I'm here on my own with Cap and a lot of space. Also, the security is good." He added the security part as if it was an afterthought, but at the end of the day, I felt safe in this house.

"That's fine with me, I appreciate it, but we'll be out of your hair soon."

He turned to look at me, and I caught the movement out of the corner of my eye and met his gaze.

"There's no rush," he murmured. "I like having you both here, and Cap has never been happier."

"We won't outstay our welcome." He tried to stand, and winced, then held out a hand.

"Help me up, will you?"

I couldn't move fast enough, anything to help him. He grasped my hand and stood, and then he was there kissing me thoroughly until I was so heated that I felt as if I'd come in my pants just from kissing.

If he was this good at a simple kiss, then fuck knows what he would be like in bed.

Game over. If I didn't get away from here now, then I'd demand to find out, and I pulled away.

"Good night," I said, then went in and lifted Daisy from the sofa, taking her upstairs, tucking her in, taking a cold shower, and getting into bed, burying my face in a pillow, before silently losing my shit.

The next few days I spent attempting to avoid alone time with Leo, and he spent his time finding me.

He kissed me in the kitchen, the garden, the front room, and even out on our walks with Cap and Daisy.

And hell if I thought this would ever happen, but I was kissing him back.

A FEW DAYS LATER, a little after nine, Eric turned up at the house. He didn't knock, just walked straight in with great purpose, another man behind him, and two children trailing them. When Eric stopped dead in the doorway to the kitchen, everyone piled up after him, but somehow they all managed to get past until the kitchen was full of people.

"We brought our swimming stuff, Uncle Leo," the girl said.

Leo ruffled her hair, before high-fiving the slightly older boy who was with her. I recognized them from the event at the firehouse, two kids, their dad, sitting with Eric, and watching me get an award I hadn't even wanted. Eric's partner, the same man who'd visited me in the hospital, and hugged me at the event, now shook my hand and gave me a side hug, and then with a nod to Eric, he and the kids went directly into the garden. They noticed Daisy, who was in the corner with the hedgehog family, and that was a good thing because I didn't want her in here while I talked to Eric. When she happily went onto the patio with them and Cap and left me with Eric and Leo, I felt I could tell as many lies as I needed to in order to get Eric to leave without questioning me.

I held out a hand to Eric to shake, and he took it, but then, to my surprise, he pulled me into a bro-hug, complete with slapping my back, which freaking hurt, because Eric is a big guy, and my ribs still ached like a bitch. When we parted, he held me away from him and then glanced from me to Leo with a thoughtful expression.

"What's happened?" he asked us, or rather he was asking Leo, and I bit my tongue instead of launching into an explanation.

"He needed a place to stay for him and his daughter, Daisy," Leo began, and looked to me for help on what to say next. At that moment, something shifted between us because he was willing to keep my secrets even from his best friend, the same man I'd come to for help in the first place. The last thing I wanted was to come between the two of them, but what did Eric need to know now? Leo had said I could stay, he'd heard what he needed to hear and he hadn't judged me, but could I face going through it all again.

"Turns out it hurts when you get beaten up," I bordered on dismissive, but Eric's eyes narrowed.

"Jesus, tell me who I need to kill," Eric snapped.

Leo touched Eric's arm, "No one, the guy's in the wind, but Jason is safe here."

Eric and Leo exchanged glances, and I was sure a lot was left unsaid between them, then Eric very pointedly turned to me.

"Start from the beginning."

I snorted a laugh. Really? He wanted me to go that far back? Then I sobered because maybe Leo deserved to know what it was that had driven me to keep Daisy safe, and if Leo knew, then Eric would know, anyway.

"I was seventeen when I first broke the law," I began, and couldn't fail to see Leo's eyes widen. "I guess I shouldn't be telling a cop that," I added, but he waved it off, and for some reason, I felt comfortable that he'd ignore all the past shit.

Why? Because he kissed you? Because he passionately promised to look out for Daisy? You're a fucking idiot, Banks.

"Before then, I was pretty much a straight-A student, but at sixteen I came out to my family as bi, or at least, they found out after they caught me with our neighbors' nephew visiting from San Fran, and things weren't good with them after that." It seemed as if I didn't have to go into any more details when Leo spoke.

"Ash, Sean's husband, had a similar thing happen to him. Not everyone has flowers and parties as a kid."

"Yeah, so it was no skin off my nose," I lied. "I had a skill with computers, hacked enough money from my parents' accounts to leave, and that it was it, my first law-breaking." I decided it was enough to consign my fucked-up family to the footnotes of this big reveal and pressed ahead. "So there's me at seventeen, I'm playing in this crappy band in the ass-end of nowhere, and I *changed* some things for people who paid." I air quoted *changed* because it encompassed a lot more than I could ever explain. "I needed money, and so I went into accounts, hacked my way around, got parking tickets reversed, grades changed, small fry, which is what it would have stayed, but I met Daisy's mom, Rain."

"She's currently in the hospital in a coma," Leo filled in.

Eric's eyes widened. "Really? In a coma?"

"Yep," I said when Leo just nodded.

"Wait, did you hack something for her?" Eric asked.

I laughed hollowly. "She had this trust account from her grandfather or something, with what seemed like so much money until the day it inevitably ran out, so yeah I did." I realized where I was going with all of this, and I got up and closed the door, in case Daisy came back in and heard anything. All being well, one day, I'd tell her everything I could, but right now, her mom was at the center of who she was, and I refused to destroy that. "She walked into this shitty little gig I was playing, covers of old songs from eighties hair bands, and I was *alive*. She was fifteen. I guess she was everything I needed right then because we'd both lost lives we knew. She was life and fire, and we both got so damn high." I lowered my voice even more at that part, which was one of the more shameful episodes of my teenage life.

I waited for Leo's reaction, expecting disgust, or remonstration; instead, he was curious.

"So, Rain was your girlfriend?"

"Rain? No, Jesus, she was out of my league. She ended up with the lead singer of our band, and I was in this hot and heavy thing with Micky-J, the bass player, anyway." I tapped my fingers on my thigh in a recognizable rhythm, the drumline to some eighties song. "I was the drummer, always the weird one, and so obviously into guys for the most part. Bi, I guess, but tending toward guys."

"And?"

"Somehow, because of Rain, I got involved in shit I

should never have started, but she had this way about her, and she just wanted what was owed her. It was so messed up." I ran a hand through my hair to give myself time to think.

"Drugs?" Eric prompted as I paused.

"No, not me, but at that moment, I felt I was owed something from life as well. So what better way to do that than to fuck over her father. In my defense, I didn't really know who or what he was, just that he had stopped sending her money, which was enough when I was young, smoked a lot of weed, lost my way, and didn't have a fucking clue what I was getting into. I was naive, made mistakes, and then Rain..."

I laced my hands in my lap, not knowing what else to do with them that didn't involve tapping a crazy slamming beat on my thigh.

"Rain what?"

"... she was in and out of my life, over the years, taking whatever money I managed to divert from her father's holding companies, nothing big, a couple thousand or so here and there, nothing that any millionaire would notice. Right?"

I couldn't help the snort of derision, damn right I'd been naïve.

"What happened?" Eric asked.

"Rain's father found me, and that was the end of things." I wondered if I would get away with leaving it at that.

Leo pressed on, "Found you, how?"

Evidently, this wasn't being left at all. "Turns out, I wasn't as clever as I'd thought. I had no comprehension of the reach of the man when he sat me down in his office and asked me what the fuck I'd been doing and how the hell I thought I'd get away with it. He gave me a choice then, I either work for him, or I don't. But the 'don't' part came with a price tag where I might end up being forever buried in the cement foundations of a parking lot."

"Jesus," Eric cursed.

"Yeah, he didn't help. That was the day it all started. Silas threatened to pull Rain back into his life, and I knew it would kill her to be part of that. I saw him for who he was, all the things he'd hidden away under a cloak of respectability, and I also saw how much Rain hated him and understood why. So when she came to me telling me that after one night's drunken hook-up—one, that was all —we were having a baby, and wanting to leave, I planned things, wanted to give her and the baby a new life. You know, live up to my responsibilities."

"What did you do?"

"I planned to hack his accounts, move a small amount of money around, get away and start over again."

"Did you love her?" Leo asked, and I met his gaze steadily.

"No."

"But you did steal money for her and your unborn baby."

"Things didn't go according to plan and it was Rain who screwed everything up. The irony was that this time, it wasn't *me* who stole money from Silas."

"Wait." This time, it was Leo who leaned forward, a hundred connections coming to one inevitable conclusion. "You admitted to embezzling from iTech—"

"Which is one of Silas' shell corporations, not that

you'd know unless you dug further. The same one I'd been stealing from for years."

"—and it wasn't you. Who was it?" He stared at me. "Rain?"

I left out a humorless laugh then because my one act of honor, which had been fueled mostly by the unfounded belief she was making a better life for our unborn baby, had left me vulnerable and willing to take the fall.

"She had access to my software, knew what she was doing, but she never meant it maliciously. She wasn't deliberately trying to get me arrested, but when someone lifts a quarter million from a company in audit season, you get noticed. She left and made it to Vermont, sent me a letter, told me we had a daughter that she'd named Daisy because she said they were a hopeful flower. I wasn't going to let Rain take the fall, and I thought at least my daughter would be safe."

"Hill Valley, right? Where she met this Billy guy," Leo commented, and I realized he knew things I thought I'd have to explain.

"Yeah. I never got to follow, I was arrested, took the fall, and it was the right thing to do because I would've done anything to keep our unborn baby safe." I stared at Leo, daring him to say otherwise.

"What I don't get is, why did she come back here?"

"The money ran out, that's all I can think."

"Shit."

Shit was right. "Then it's my last day in prison." I pinched my fingers together, leaving a little gap. "I was this close to the final gate, and this guy Austin, clearly a cop in a suit, calls me into a room. They're trying to build a case against Silas, need my hacking skills to get in through the backdoors I'd built in his software to get evidence, blah blah. And oh, did I know that Rain had come home with Daisy and that Billy had followed from Vermont and he was an abusive asshole to Rain, and how would I like to get my ex and my baby away from everything, maybe even with a new life."

Eric sighed, "That is fucked up."

Leo spoke in a more even tone, "So, your choice was to do what they say and for them to keep an eye on Rain and Daisy, or to leave and do nothing."

"Yeah." I know I sounded aggressively fierce, but nothing was coming between Daisy and me.

"It was a non-choice," Leo said. "The burner phone, this federal agent, Austin, he gave that to you?"

"He says to sit tight. When I know it's safe, and I'm sure Billy can't find us and hurt Daisy; then we can leave."

"What if I don't want you to leave? What if what *we* have is enough to get you to stay?" Leo said with force, and Eric side-eyed him, shocked by the outburst.

"It's not our time," I was blunt.

"Are you two…?" Eric gestured between us.

"Yes," he said.

"No," I said at the same time, and Leo narrowed his eyes, but it was Eric who got us back on track.

"What about Daisy's mom?"

That was the question I'd been dreading, the part that I hadn't told Daisy, and I hunched in on myself, grief warring with determination. "Rain put Daisy in danger, let Billy into her life, looks like she took an overdose while she had Daisy in her care, and is now in a coma. I hope for Daisy's sake that she wakes up, because every child needs their mother. But… if she does, then I *will* fight her for shared custody, however shit my case is, and I will watch her with Daisy every single day of my entire fucking life."

Leo's green eyes were bright with emotion. "I know you will," he said and heaved himself up to stand, before extending a hand to me and pulling me into a hug. "And we'll help you."

Eric nodded as well, but their blind support of me wasn't something I could handle right now.

Eric held out a hand for me, and I shook it. "Meanwhile, if you need somewhere else to stay, we have a spare room that—"

"He's okay here," Leo interrupted before Eric could get out the full sentence, and Eric shook his head before punching his friend in the arm.

"So I see."

ERIC CALLED for the rest of his family, and they all trooped out, Daisy taking her place back at the hedgehog house, but Eric held back a bit, and he and Leo stopped on the porch for a good ten minutes. I had the feeling they were talking about me, and I wondered if they were all supportive to my face, but what if, out there, they were planning to dig into me and my background, or find Billy, or…

"Breathe," Leo demanded and shook my arms a little to bring me out of my little panic attack. *When did he get back in?* "Okay?" he asked after a short while when I shrugged away from him, suddenly afraid that I couldn't trust anything about him.

"We can go," I blurted, because shit, I wasn't going to let Billy back in our lives right now.

"Woah, where did that come from?"

My insecurities and lack of trust. "Nothing, ignore me."

"I'd love you and Daisy to stay."

I glanced over at Daisy, who was cuddled up with Cap, looking at one of the many picture books that Leo had in the room. She was so happy here, smiling, she had Cap, books, even those damn hedgehogs she loved.

"I'm sorry," I said a little desperately and hoped he believed me.

He tugged me back out of the kitchen and crutched into the hallway, pulled the door shut, and pressed me against it, so there was no way of Daisy pushing out, then. I didn't like that. I wanted Daisy to be able to get to me if she needed me, even if right now she was happy as a bee in a flower with that book and with Cap, but all he wanted to do was talk.

"I want you to believe me," he said, and cradled my face. "Believe that I want you here, and that I would do anything to keep you safe."

What could I say?

"I believe you," I murmured. And it was only as I said the words that I realized I half believed them.

THE TENSION between us was torture. As he made dinner he kept brushing past me, touching my shoulder, letting his hand linger, as if he couldn't imagine not touching me. By the time that Daisy was in bed, and he tugged me into the dark hallway downstairs I was ready to kiss him again and it was me who initiated the first kiss.

We made out like two kids on a first date, learning the

lines of each other even as he shuffled a little to get his leg comfortable. He cradled my face, supported me, then kissed me hard and fast, messy and dirty, and I was hard in an instant. All the insecurities and fears fled from my mind, and in their place was this mantra of need, want, now. He moved a little, and I felt him just as hard, and then he pressed a hand between us, dragging at my shorts, then his, until I was gloriously bare against him, and I rutted as we kissed, chasing the need to come, needing more kisses, more pressure, more of everything.

I fell into my orgasm with a cry muffled in the kiss, and he followed me as we breathed against each other's mouths, silently staring into my eyes, and I was lost.

"Please stay," he murmured. "I want to keep you both safe,"

We slept separately, and he never pushed for me to go into his room, although the kiss we shared outside on the landing, with Cap between us, was intense. When I shut the door behind me, I leaned against it for the longest time and I knew one thing for sure.

My heart would never be safe while I stayed here.

NINETEEN

Leo
_____

SOMEHOW, we were at twelve days since Jason and Daisy had arrived, and I couldn't help hoping they stayed twelve more. There was no sign of Billy; I had Bella keeping an eye on things, and this Austin guy on the other end of Jason's burner phone said that it was probable that he'd gone to ground. So in one way, he could do what he wanted now, he could go off to the East Coast where he told me he had a family. But I didn't think he could move out, and it seemed like he agreed.

There was also a glimmer of news from Austin in that Daisy's mom was showing signs of brain activity, which suggested she might make it out of the coma. Still, the story when it had come in an hour ago had caused Jason to spiral down into silence, and it was this quiet I was facing now. He watched Daisy play with the hedgehog family, which was Mia's favorite as well. There was an entire collection of the characters I could buy, and I may have gone out and bought every single one for Mia, although I wouldn't admit that to Sean and Asher, who already said I spoiled her too much.

Pfft, that was my job as honorary uncle.

Anyway, now Daisy was playing with them as well, although where Mia stared at them a lot, forcing them in nooks and crannies of the big house they came with, Daisy had a complicated hierarchy and cute storylines that I could've listened to for days. At the moment, a tea party had ended, and Lulu was getting into trouble because she hadn't washed up, but when the cute little story turned a weird corner, I leaned forward in my chair and watched a little closer.

"Do it or trouble," Daisy said and flicked Lulu over with her finger, making little crying noises for the tiny character.

"That's not very nice for poor Lulu," I said and twisted awkwardly to sit on the floor next to her. I expected to teach a valuable life lesson right there, using my best uncle's voice to encourage her to work things out with her characters. Only she stared at me, blue eyes wet with tears, and all I could do was hold out my arms and offer her a hug. She didn't hesitate, climbing there and clinging to me. I wasn't sure if she was still crying, but the way she held me had a quiet desperation, and I wasn't going to let her go anytime soon. Cap came over to investigate, pushing at her arm with his nose, and then leaning on me, and then I had a lapful of little girl and dog.

Jason came in from the kitchen, wiping his hands on a cloth, a smile on his face as he looked down at me, but he sobered when I shook my head, then crouched down on the other side from Cap. He smoothed blonde curls from Daisy's face, and she caught his gaze.

"Can you tell Daddy what's up, pumpkin?" he said, and I waited for her to move from me to him.

"Mommy was sad all the time, and Daddy-B was mean," she whispered against my shirt, so low it was difficult to hear her. Jason sat down next to me then, pressed himself against my side, and leaned closer.

"Was Daddy-B mean to you as well?" Jason asked after a small pause where it was apparent he was pulling himself together. This was a question that I'd wanted to ask Daisy, and I think the weight of it was heavy on his shoulders as well.

"No, I got presents, but I had to be quiet. All the time."

I guess to a three-year-old, a present was a good way to buy affection. I mean, look at me and the fabulous hedgehog and country house collection. Not to mention the hedgehog stables, hotel, and craft village buildings I had wrapped up for Mia for this Christmas. Not that I needed to buy her gifts for her to love me, her Uncle Fido was cool, and she loved me big time.

"And Mommy cried?" Jason encouraged.

"All the time, and then she didn't have money 'coz Daddy-B had it, and she slept and was all funny."

Funny didn't necessarily mean that she cracked jokes, and I picked my way through what she'd said, following the points and drawing conclusions that could've been unfounded or not. One thing I was thankful for was that Billy hadn't hurt Daisy, or at least not physically abused her, but he'd clearly hurt her mom and then stolen Rain's money, which led to what? Was she trapped then, did it make her ill, or were drugs involved? After all, she was in the hospital having overdosed so that assumption could've been true.

"I don't want to cry," she blurted, and sat back from me, scrubbing at her eyes, seeming a lot older than her nearly-four years.

"It's okay to cry," Jason said, but I heard the grief in his voice and instinct made me want to get between him and Daisy and make them smile.

"But it's also okay to be excited about Christmas, and your birthday, and feeding Cap. What would you like for your birthday?"

"A puppy," she said solemnly. "One just like Cap. And a kitten."

I nodded as if I was considering the options. "How about more hedgehogs for the collection here instead?"

She shook her head. "They're not mine. I can't keep them when we go."

I fought back the instinct to say that she didn't have to go and that she and Jason could stay for a while longer, but realistically there wasn't anything here that meant Jason would stay. Once Billy was found, they could go where he wanted, start a new life anywhere. Right now, though, I hugged her, loved that Jason was right next to me, scratched behind Cap's ear, and tried not to think about what the future held.

Tomorrow was Thanksgiving dinner with my family, which I'd told Jason would be quiet.

I lied.

———

"THESE LOOK NEW," Jason poked around in the bags that Asher had just dropped off. They probably were, but I wasn't going to say that.

"You needed something for Thanksgiving."

"I could have gone to Goodwill, and I have some money left—"

"Asher always buys clothes and doesn't wear them," I interrupted because I wanted to clear that frown from his face.

"Hmmm," Jason sounded disbelieving as he pulled out a baby-soft blue short-sleeved shirt. "These don't look like second hand at all."

I shrugged and decided that not talking was my best strategy. Only Jason looked so confused.

"Ash is around the same size as you and was clearing out his closet, and you needed clothes, it's a win/win."

He pulled chinos from the bag and held them out in front of him. "This still has the label on."

"Maybe he didn't like them."

Jason picked up the bags and placed them at the bottom of the stairs, then came back in holding up something that really wouldn't fit him at all. The dress was Daisy-sized, a bright pink princess dress on a tiny hanger with the Disney label on the side.

"And he bought this but didn't want to wear it?" Jason suggested with a healthy dose of sarcasm.

Ah, he'd found the dress I'd bought for Daisy. I waggled my eyebrows. "Who knows what Ash and Sean get up to behind closed doors."

He gathered the pink froth of material to his chest. "I'll thank him when I see him next, but right now, for Daisy, thank *you*."

"Why are you thanking me?" I blinked as innocently as I could, but he shook his head. "Okay, then." I was embarrassed about the way he looked at me, seeing right through my schemes, so I fell back on what I did best. Organization. "The cab will be here in a couple of hours, and you'd better take that dress up to Daisy and wake her up."

The next time I saw Jason, shaved, wearing the chinos and shirt, and Daisy next to him in the dress, I felt so many emotions, it was difficult to pin them down.

"You look beautiful, Daisy," I said, and made an exaggerated bow in front of her.

"Daddy says I'm a princess," Daisy said and twirled in her tiny pink ballet shoes until she dropped into a heap next to Cap. He wouldn't be coming today, too much chaos, and too many children who'd want to tease him rather than love him, but he was still sporting the purple bow that Daisy had insisted he wear for this special day.

Jason watched from the bottom step, a fond smile on his face, lost in thought, and I stood in front of him, my back to Daisy.

"You look amazing," I said.

He pushed at his hair, which was getting longer by the day. When he'd arrived all scruffy, he'd attempted everything to tidy himself up, and we'd planned to go to the barbers, only Daisy needed her hair cut as well. Both of us had put it off, sticking to walks in the park and the valley behind, never too far from the house, and always alert.

"I'd say that I was going to thank Ash for the clothes, but you got them, didn't you?"

I couldn't quite meet his gaze. "Maybe."

He touched my cheek, and I stared right at him.

"Thank you."

I pressed my hand over his, and he stiffened and was

surprised. "I want to kiss you," I murmured, and didn't expect a reply, only after a small sigh, he did.

"However wrong it is, I want to kiss you, too."

That confused me. "Why is it wrong?"

He huffed and shook his head. "An ex-con on the road to the East Coast as soon as it's safe, and a cop whose entire life is in San Diego? How would that work?"

I wished I had answers, but I didn't have time to think of any because the cabdriver laid on his horn, and in a few minutes, we were heading to Mama's. Jason sat in the back seat, but he didn't once question where the booster seat for Daisy had come from when I'd pulled it out of the garage. I'd scuffed it up a bit, even unpicked some of the topstitching, made it look as if it had been someone else's, but as he belted her in, he caught me watching and smiled.

"I didn't think of this." He sounded angry at himself. "I should have."

"I'm used to Mia," I replied, and wished I hadn't said anything when Jason's smile dropped. I could have kicked myself because, of course, he wasn't *used* to Daisy at all.

The journey was only thirty minutes, and we arrived just after midday, and well after the start of the ball game. Jason and Daisy stayed behind me at first, and I know that the family is a lot to take in. Not to mention the huge Christmas Tree that was always up for Thanksgiving, plus the garlands and glitter that was everywhere. But, in the scrimmage of cousins' children, Daisy was soon encouraged away, mainly when Lizzie, the youngest daughter of a second cousin, had the same dress and announced that she and Daisy would be princesses together. When Jason and I, at last, made our way to Mama's empire, past my dad, who was glued to the game,

I found Lorna on a stool, and Reid stirring something in a huge saucepan.

"Hi guys, I want you to meet Jason," I said, and three sets of eyes settled on me, and then Jason. Mama moved first, bustling around the others and pulling Jason into a patented Mama hug. Think of all the stereotypes of an Italian matriarch, and you have Mama Byrne, married to my papa, a cop the same as me, now retired. What she loved was a house full of people, and that included the entire extended family. An extended family made up of a lot of cops, most of my uncles, a couple of my aunts, my brother, cousins… we had the local precincts covered, which was a standing joke every year.

"So good to *finally* meet you in person," she said.

I winced internally because that was her subtle way of suggesting I should have brought him over earlier. Given he'd only been in my life a couple of weeks, I was ready to defend my position, but this was the Mama-Byrne show, and she wasn't to know that we'd not got a back story that went back years. "We owe you so much for Eric," she added and held him so hard he was pinned.

Oh yeah, apart from that connection where he saved Eric.

"He's handsome," she patted Jason's cheek and let out a torrent of Italian, which he had no hope of following, and when he glanced at me to translate, all I could do was shrug. "And I want to meet little Daisy, but after dinner, so I can meet her properly?"

"Yes, ma'am," he replied, and she tutted.

"Call me Mama, none of this 'yes, ma'am'."

"Okay," then it was my siblings' turn to hug Jason, but there was a conspicuous absence.

"Where's Jax?"

"Not here," Mama said, and turned back to her cooking.

Lorna shrugged, Reid raised his eyebrows in a shared *what the fuck*, and I decided discretion was the better part of valor where a disappointed Mama was concerned and dropped the subject. That didn't stop me sending a quick text to Jax, as Jason and Reid discussed today's game, both of them clearly knowing nothing about football at all, with my own version of *where in hell are you?*

What was more worrying was that the answer I got back was a mysterious apology that read: *In Vancouver, sorry.* I stealthily showed the reply to Reid and Lorna but pocketed my phone when Mama looked my way.

The Byrne siblings didn't miss Thanksgiving. It was the law. But I didn't have much time to think about it, apart from missing Jax like a limb, because his ex and my nieces were here, and I visited with them until I was called back to the kitchen, where Dad was now standing by the centerpiece, ready to carry it in. This was my one memory of Thanksgiving, the mismatched and borrowed tables, the different-sized chairs, the kids' table, the grown-ups' table, and the extra seating for anyone who turned up, which this year included Jason and Daisy. I made a point of suggesting that Daisy sit with her dad, but she'd made fast friends with the extended Byrne family kids, and that was it.

There was nothing about her that was as reticent as she'd been when she first arrived at my house, and Lillian had visited a few more times. That Daisy didn't like Billy was visible, but not for any upset to her, he hadn't hurt her physically, but the fact that he'd made Rain cry pulled out the protective side of Daisy. Lillian wanted to talk more, and Jason had given his permission that would last right up until he left.

That damn expiration date was haunting me, but staring at Jason didn't help, because he was sitting right in front of me, sandwiched between Mama and Reid, and I caught him looking at me all confused. I pulled my shit together and winked, and then we held hands to say grace.

I had a complicated relationship with God. I was Catholic on paper, but the word *practicing* was something I left out of the description. I was an Easter/Christmas kind of guy, leaving my prayers for times when I found quiet. I would visit the church every so often, go through the procedures, immerse myself in the colorful language, larger-than-life characters, and I often found the solitude of losing myself in prayer if the church was empty, but the social side of the church wasn't for me. I was all about quiet and faith and good deeds, at least that was how Father Nicholls had described me when I'd gone to him in confusion at fourteen after I'd kissed my first boy.

I was the only one of the four Byrne siblings who'd ever attended church with Mama and Papa, the other three had varying beliefs, stretching from atheist to spiritual, but never once did our parents make us think any of us were wrong in our convictions. Still, we all held hands now on Thanksgiving because we were family, and I sent a quick prayer at the end of giving thanks for the food.

Let Jason find his way. Keep them safe. Let Jason and Daisy stay.

After all, I wanted them to stay, and yeah, God would know what I felt.

"You must go home and put the tree up!" Mama

exclaimed suddenly and very loudly, and I instinctively knew that she'd cornered the conversation with Jason. Daisy was there as well, standing by her dad, grinning up at Mama and visibly vibrating with excitement. "They tell me your tree isn't up yet."

"Not all of us put our trees up in November, Mama," Reid tried to back me up, but it was a losing battle.

"Can we do the tree at home?" she asked, and Jason looked helpless, caught in the web of a woman who loved decorating the house, and the hope in his daughter's eyes. I swallowed the emotion at the way she used the word *home*.

"We'll do the tree on the weekend," I said immediately, because no one was breaking Daisy's heart, not on my watch. No one was more surprised than me when Daisy scampered around the table and yanked me back from the table to hug me.

"Thank you, thank you, thank you," she shouted, and then went back for the rest of her dinner, probably explaining why she was so excited, given that the Byrne kids were all listening to her with rapt attention. My heart melted when I watched her, and I even had the urge to wish that she and Jason could be here for Christmas.

When we left my old family home, weighed down with leftovers and an entire uneaten pie, we were quiet in the cab, Daisy falling asleep. I was in the front again, but I reached a hand back, anything to reassure myself that Jason was okay. He laced his fingers with mine and leaned forward, and like that, we made it home in no time at all, all the while holding hands.

What did that mean? I'd wanted to touch him. I wanted to kiss him, and the heat that had built inside me had nowhere to go. I couldn't imagine a future without him, I feared for him and Daisy, I wanted them in my life, wanted him in my bed. I needed to make hot chocolate, put a tree up, write cards together, and a hundred other things.

And all I could think was that maybe this was what falling in love was like.

TWENTY

Jason

WHEN WE ARRIVED HOME, Leo juggled all the food, and I carried Daisy indoors, taking her up to bed. She stirred long enough to use the bathroom and brush her teeth, and I helped her out of the princess dress, hanging it in the small closet that was hers and filled almost entirely with pink.

"Daddy?" she murmured as I tucked her into her side of the bed, moving the pillow fort, so she had enough room.

"Yes, sweetheart."

"I love you," she said with a yawn.

"I love you, too," I pressed a kiss to her curls and smiled in the semi-darkness.

"An' I love Cap, and Leo, and Mom." She turned on her side and was asleep before I could even answer her. I could've gotten into bed myself, it was nine p.m., and I could've gotten a book and read under the tiny bedside lamp, or I could go downstairs and face the tension that had been building between Leo and myself. Thoughts of us getting off together in the hallway consumed me, and the idea of kissing him didn't scare me; in fact, it had been all I'd thought about all day. When Daisy had run to him, hugging him for saying that we'd put up the tree, something inside me snapped open.

I think it was another frozen part of me cracking wide open and letting in affection and love.

I *know* it was my heart.

When I went downstairs, Leo was on the sofa, his leg up on a stool, and he was massaging his left hip.

"Are you okay?" I asked, and he gestured to the hot chocolate on the coffee table.

"There's one for you," he said and continued to press at the muscles. "And yeah, aching from being off-balance is all." I picked up the hot chocolate, and instead of taking the opposite seat, I sat next to Leo. There was no point in playing coy, I wanted to kiss him, and maybe more, and I needed it tonight.

Just one good memory of what I could have had if my life had been different.

Only he was in pain, and I knew something about that. "You want me to have a look?" I asked, and when he nodded cautiously, I placed my drink on the table. "Turn your back to me," I instructed, and he did the best he could, and within seconds, I'd found the trigger point in his hip, and he inhaled sharply. "Can you lie down?" I asked and moved back to watch him wriggle and curse until he was lying on his belly on the long leather sectional. "You're really tense," I observed, and tugged his loose pants down a little to get to the dimples in his back just above the cleft of his round, entirely perfect, ass. I'd become interested in anatomy when I was in prison, borrowed every book I could find, and even had the nebulous idea that even if I couldn't become a firefighter, I could do massage therapy, or learn to be a chiropractor. I could maybe work with first responders in recovery.

Not that this would happen, with my record I wasn't going to get a job anywhere, but I was good with my hands, I could do casual work and earn money that way—

"Earth to Jason?" Leo interrupted my daydreaming.

I began to move my hands, tracing the muscles and pressing to ascertain which trigger points I needed to work, and where the pain originated. It soon became apparent when Leo hissed under his breath. For a second, I kneaded the area around the pain center and then moved closer, pressing on the knot and holding my fingers still, cutting the blood supply to the offending muscle so that it could restart and reshape. Leo tensed and then finally relaxed, and I carried on until he began to hum a Christmas carol, and then I knew that I'd done what I could because the pain must have eased, and I helped him to sit up. I was kneeling next to him and waiting for him to tell me if he felt better when he tugged me hard and I overbalanced, ending up sprawled across him. I scrabbled to find purchase, but he held me off balance and then kissed me, and I had no option but to melt into his hold.

Somehow he moved, or I moved, hell if I know. I was straddling him, and I could feel the rigid length of him against my cock. I groaned and pleaded into the kiss, and we rocked as we kissed, and I wanted more. Then he pulled back and cradled my face and stopped moving.

"Are we doing this again?" he asked tentatively. I recalled the kiss in the hallway, where I rutted and strained against him just to feel something.

"Do you want to?"

He huffed a small laugh. "I've wanted to since I saw you in the hospital the day after you saved Eric."

"That was just gratitude."

He stole another heated kiss. "Maybe, but it wasn't gratitude when I kissed you in the bathroom, which still wasn't my finest moment."

"Nor mine," I whispered against his lips. I wanted all of him with a desperation that made it hard to breathe, and I wished he'd stop talking.

"And it wasn't gratitude when we were in the hallway. Or the moments when I watch you, or the way I have to keep taking cold showers so that I can come downstairs halfway decent."

"Oh—"

"It isn't gratitude when I hear you reading to Daisy, or when I think what life would be like if you and Daisy were my family."

"Leo, fuck—"

"I want you and Daisy to stay here forever."

"Are you high? Leo—"

"I'm falling for you so hard," he muttered.

Before I could pull back and question all that he'd just said, he kissed me again, and then I couldn't think at all. I loved that when I pushed my hands under his shirt and rubbed at his nipples, then pinched them, he moaned and arched into the touch. But add in the fact he was a toppy bastard who wasn't entirely happy that I was the one sitting on him and I was in heaven. I wanted someone else to take me high, wanted to be able to trust Leo with everything... to tell me what to do. He took me right to the edge, frantic and needy, pushing his hands into my shorts, yanking them down as best he could, then begging me to do the same to him, until we were bare against each other. He took hold of both us as best he could and I arched over him, lifted myself on my knees, straddling him, the material of my shorts digging into my legs, and in a smooth motion, he lifted me higher, and between us, I was finally naked, and then so was he.

This is what I wanted, right here, at this moment, I needed this orgasm so badly, and fuck, I was so close.

You keep me safe. You look after Daisy. I'm falling for you. I didn't care if I was doing this for the wrong reasons, if it was gratitude or just raw lust, but I sealed my lips to his, thrusting into our joined hands until the boiling need inside me erupted, and I was coming so hard my brain stopped working. At least it felt that way, as he joined me, groaning his release, and deepening the kiss until it was frantic, and then it stilled and became gentle until it was nothing more than us breathing together.

I thought it would take a Christmas miracle for me to feel safe. But to feel safe and wanted all at the same time? That was bigger than what I'd wished for. And twice as scary.

We cleaned up quietly, and then he tugged me upstairs, and wrapped naked together we fell asleep.

MY BURNER PHONE WOKE ME; it was never far from me, and it was there on his nightstand vibrating and moving on the glass top. Blearily, I reached for it as memories of last night assailed me, and I was very close to dropping the damn thing.

What the hell have I done?

I'd let down every barrier, acted on nothing but lust,

just because he'd looked at me as if I was special? What kind of fucking idiot was I?

Then Leo saying that Daisy and I could stay forever? Who even used words like that anymore? There was no forever, so what kind of fairytale did he think we were living in?

"An idiot falling for someone who he can never be with," I muttered to the phone as I opened it and stared at the blurry words on the screen.

Have a possible lead on Billy.

I rolled up from his bed, put on my shorts and pocketed my cell, all very carefully so as not to wake up Leo, who had murmured something and then hidden his face with a pillow. For the longest time, I stared down at him, willing him to wake up so I could talk to him, but when his breathing stayed even and deep, I headed to my room, catching that it was only five a.m., and tiptoeing past Daisy and into the bathroom.

I had no idea when distrust around Leo had become trust, or when anger and fear had become a passion and need, or even the particular moment when attraction had become much, *much*, more. All I did know was that I was hiding in my shower, with the door locked, and I had no idea what I'd done, and I felt a hundred kinds of wrong for going straight into panic mode.

Talk to Leo. Tell him everything. Make him part of this mess in your head and get him to help. He was tired last night, and he probably didn't mean half of it. No one tells the truth when they're making love.

"Sex!" I exclaimed and realized I was talking to the tiles now. "It's just sex."

It's certainly not a future of any kind and he wouldn't

be part of whatever new life I was going to start on the East Coast. Yeah, I couldn't ask the cop with the friendly family, beautiful house, steady career, and the best of friends, to move a thousand miles to the opposite side of the country. That wouldn't go down well.

He'd probably think I was a freak when he woke up and saw I'd run from the bedroom like a cat with his tail on fire. Even though I knew he'd immediately think I was up looking out for Daisy, part of him would know he'd scared me. Last night wasn't only lust, or passion, or fire, but worst of all, he'd offered me hope, and for a moment, I could imagine our little family and that hope had burned bright inside me.

Until it hit me, it was never going to happen.

"I need to talk to him." I wasn't the kind of person to run from confrontation, or at least I'd never been before. Turning off the water, I then rough-dried my hair and wrapped a towel around my waist, and with a deep inhalation of breath, I moved past Daisy, who was nothing more than a few golden curls peeking out from her covers. Then, with determination, I opened my door and came face to face with a stranger peering right back at me, and for a second, all I could think was that this was someone Billy had sent, and I let out an unmanly yelp.

"Whoa, whoa," the man said, and I recognized him from a photo in a grouping on the stairs. "You the new boyfriend?" the guy asked and crossed his arms over his chest. He looked me up and down, and I saw the moment his gaze alighted on the scars on my arm, but I didn't move. I was lost for words, because first of all, I was wearing nothing but a towel, and second any minute now,

Leo was going to walk out of the bedroom, probably in less than a towel, and this could get super weird.

"Who's asking?" I tilted my chin in defiance. "You an ex or something?"

The redhead snorted a laugh and relaxed a little, offering me a hand. "Jax, I'm Leo's way more handsome and significantly younger brother." Jax was the same height as me, slight and with the red hair I'd noticed first. He had a face full of freckles, and a firm handshake, and he was wearing a suit and tie. Wasn't he a builder? Why was he was in a suit?

"Hi," I said lamely, wishing I was wearing more than a towel.

"Where is he?"

"Who?"

"Leo," Jax said and tilted his head at me. "Unless he's undercover and he's given you a different name—"

Jax shuffled forward as Leo, thankfully in sweats and a T, came out of his room and cuffed him upside the head.

"If I was undercover, asshole, then you just blew it for me."

Jax shoved his brother back, "That's okay, I'll take this criminal and handcuff him to your bed," he joke-leered, and then snorted a laugh as he and Leo tussled against the wall, roughhousing as brothers did. I stepped back once, then another, until I was inside my room, with the ability to shut the door if I needed. I quickly pulled on shorts and a soft coral-colored T-shirt, running my fingers through my wet hair and wishing I could turn back time to last night, maybe a few minutes before the best orgasm of my life.

Right to the moment before Leo told us we could stay, and before I felt like everything was going wrong.

TWENTY-ONE

Leo

"HEY, HOP-ALONG, CAN WE TALK?" Jax asked as soon as Jason walked away.

I loved my brother, despite the fact he was an ass, but it was actually Jason I wanted to talk to right now. About how what I said last night was completely real. I could see the tension in Jason, and we needed to talk. Whatever was going on with Jax, it was Jason who consumed my thoughts.

"Can we talk later?" I asked with impatience. "And who let you in?"

He frowned at me. "I have a key, moron. What crawled up your butt and died?"

"I've got something going on here, Jax."

"Well, I have a real lead on Z," Jax murmured so low that I didn't catch it at first, and then it hit me.

"What?"

"Someone in Vancouver reached out... I was there yesterday, Vancouver, I met this guy who says Z married his sister and he's…" Jax scrubbed at his hair. "He could still be in Canada."

I clapped a hand to Jax's shoulder, not wanting to say that this could possibly be another dead end. "That's awesome news."

I heard Jason and Daisy's door shut, aware I'd lost the chance to talk to Jason right now; still, there was always later, and I was determined to make Jason see that we had something that could be more.

"Where's the coffee?" Jax asked, bright-eyed, and bushy-tailed, whereas I felt exhausted.

"You make it, and I'll be down in a minute."

"And we can add the notes to the case?"

"Yep."

Jax always got excited about that part, but clues and trails in a case were only exciting for me when they panned out. This was the tenth city Jax had gone to, looking for his twin brother Zachariah, or as he remembered calling him, Z. They'd been split up at a young age and Z had dropped out of the system, no one knew if he was still in Canada, or if he'd ended up in the US as Jax had.

All I knew was that my little brother needed my help, and even though I wanted desperately to clear the air with Jason, it was Jax who had to come first right now.

By the time he left, we'd drunk so much coffee, I was buzzing, and even though it was nine a.m., there was no sign of Daisy or her dad. So, me being me, I went to find them, with toast, coffee, orange juice, and Cap.

Cap was my secret weapon. No one could say no to him, which was how I made it inside the bedroom, and ended up on my own with Jason, given that Daisy was in the bath, and Cap wanted to play with the bubbles.

"About last night—"

"Let's not talk—"

We started talking at the same time, but there was no way I was responding to his request not to talk. Instead, I took his hand, which wasn't what he'd been expecting. He tugged back at first, but I wasn't arguing with this, and I laced our fingers.

I got straight to the point. "Is it so impossible to think you can stay here?"

He frowned at me. "Yeah, I need to make a life for Daisy, somewhere that maybe Rain can come to if she's able to."

I stepped closer, could see the darker blue in his eyes I was that close. "Do you still want to be with Rain?"

"No, but if she wakes up, then I do want Rain to be in Daisy's life."

"Then she can move in here," I announced with dramatic flair, not entirely thinking everything through.

He shook his head. "We're not at the right time in our lives if this was another time…"

My cell rang, and I answered it without thinking, switching it speaker when I saw it was Jax.

"Not a good time—"

"Yeah, yeah, but I forgot to say, some of the order came in for Ringwood," Jax announced.

"Okay?" The children's home that Eric and Sean and I all volunteered our time at was in dire need of a new kitchen, which Eric had financed, although no one would ever know that. Adam, a former firefighter, was project managing the whole project alongside us volunteers, and I couldn't wait to start. I held tighter to Jason's hand as he attempted to pull away.

"Okay?" Jax huffed, "Earth to Turt, I have the stuff here, can you and the guys get over in January and we could make a start on the add-on?"

Jason stared right at me, looking as if he was on the verge of losing his shit even as I listened to my brother talk about things in normal life. I pressed a kiss to Jason's forehead, and he tilted his head back so we could kiss properly.

"Uh-huh," I managed to say even as Jax kept talking.

"Are you even listening to any of this?" Jax asked with a put-upon sigh, and I tried hard to focus back on what he was saying.

"Yeah?" I said, which wasn't a smart response, because it just showed I hadn't been listening at all.

"I said, can you make January?"

"This January?"

"No, 2022," Jax deadpanned. "Of course this January, idiot, otherwise I would have specified the year, moron."

That snapped me back to the here and now, "The onus is on the communicator, dickwad."

"Whatever."

"Asswipe."

"Dumbass." We sniggered then because that was what brothers did, and Jason blinked at me before smiling. "Yeah, I'll talk to Sean, but I can't speak for Eric, he's due some downtime." This conversation was surreal, and at last, Jason dropped his gaze even though he held my hand tight, and Jax kept talking.

I watched Jason pet Cap, who had come to sit next to us, bubbles all over his back, tail thumping the floor rhythmically, and one-handed, I scrolled to my calendar. There used to be a time when there'd been three schedules on there, copies of the ones held up with magnets from Torrey Pines Reserve on the fridge. Eric's one had always been slim on details because he never knew when he'd be called to a fire, and Sean's were blocked out days at a time with his job in the Emergency Department at Soledad Hospital. Now it was just mine on my phone, and on the fridge, neat, tidy, all in boxes with space to add details, looking a little forlorn right now without work on there at all but with a big circle around the fifth of January, my first day back at work, all being well. Maybe now I could add in some things for Jason and Daisy. Ballet? Swimming lessons? Or preschool? Or hell, whatever we could make of what we had here for as long as it lasted.

Please let it last for a very long time.

Like, forever. What? Where did that thought come from? Yeah, I'd fallen for Jason, but that didn't mean that he owed me anything like a forever. What we had could be quick and over in a month as soon as he felt he could move on. I pushed the worry to one side and instead attempted to focus on Jax, who was huffing again.

"I could bring some extra hands, Jason and Daisy," I saw Jason's eyes widen, and could read the expression like a book. I wanted him and Daisy to be part of my life, at least for the time being, and that meant getting out, seeing the kinds of things I did on my downtime. Also, it meant committing to something after Christmas, and that had to be worth something. Only, of course, him committing to anything post-Christmas meant acknowledging a future that he seemed terrified of.

"That would be great," Jax said, immediately, warmth and enthusiasm in his voice.

"Yeah, I'll bring help," I announced, and Jason shook his head but squeezed my hand at the same time. Somehow in all of this, maybe we could hope for normality, and that started with putting the tree up. I just wished his certainty that a future together was impossible would vanish.

At the tree lot, Daisy was in her element, Cap on his leash was somehow covered in glitter, and I was in charge. Meanwhile, Jason was doing everything he could to be on the other side of Daisy, so we couldn't talk. Finding the perfect tree was hard, but Daisy was getting into the spirit of the occasion, joining in with my silly reasons why this tree or that tree was wrong. Jason was skulking, checking around, and even though he was attempting to ignore me, he was never very far from Daisy. When we got the tree home, he began to thaw, and even though I couldn't begin to understand what was going through his head, I was determined to make him smile as we decorated.

He'd looked melancholy for most of the afternoon, uncertain, angry at times, and then in the next minute, alive and positive. It was as if he believed there was a future in this house, and allowed himself time to enjoy the thought, then for all the arguments against it to barrel into him, and leave him grieving.

Or at least, I wanted to think he might be invested in us enough to be sad that it might not happen.

"Where does this go?" Daisy interrupted my thoughts.

I crouched next to her. She was holding a tiny little drummer boy on a scarlet string, and I scooped her up in my arms so she could place it up high.

"I can play the drums," Jason said to her.

"Like for real, Daddy?" she asked and picked out the next ornament, this time a gold bauble covered in glitter.

"Yep," He tapped a rhythm on the near-empty box and finished with a flourish and a quick kiss to her head. Then she was distracted by finding all the glitter baubles she could find, and I stepped back to check the tree.

"A drummer, huh?" I asked him when he reached for more garland, and he dipped his head shyly, not something I'd ever see before.

"Yeah, I was in this band, and it wasn't sh—bad, but it wasn't good. I wanted to go on the road, you know, and explore the world, but it ended up that the farthest we ever went to was Hollywood and not even the good bit of it."

"You should take it up again."

"One day." He picked up a frosted scarlet and green apple with ornate filigree decoration, and frowned down at it. "Some of these decorations look antique."

"You mean old," I couldn't help laughing, and after a few moments, he smiled at me.

"Yeah, old, I guess."

"When her kids moved out, Mama gave us all a box of things, books, photos, and wrapped up carefully, all these ancient Christmas ornaments. They come out every year, and connect me to family."

"Yeah, I wouldn't know about that," he muttered and then shrugged. "Classic story, gay isn't right in the eyes of God, blah blah."

I wanted to pull him close and reassure him, but he was still a little prickly, and I wasn't sure what he needed was for me to tell him everything was going to be okay. How would I know if he ever contacted his family again?

"Faith is a funny thing," I said instead, "the Pope was all 'gay guys are our brothers'."

"He said it that way?" Jason teased, and I liked the lightness in him.

"Not exactly, but he says God made us the way we are, it's after that when it's all 'love the sinner, hate the sin'."

"You have religion then?" He fumbled over the words as if he couldn't quite work out how to ask me.

"I believe in my God, and I pray, and my faith keeps me centered when everything else around me has gone to shit," I said, and waited for him to laugh, or comment, or even just nod. He did none of those things and instead he looked at me thoughtfully.

"I'd like to have had that, but the church ideals my parents subscribed to weren't conducive to being gay. I mean my parents just thought I was... wait, what word did they use?" he scrunched up his nose, which was kind of adorable, although I'd never say it. "An abomination," he finished and shrugged.

"What's bom-nim-ation?" Daisy asked, and abruptly we were both aware she was listening to our every word. *Well fuck.*

"It's a snowman," Jason said, made googly eyes, then stomped his feet and growled. "An abominable snowman, and it's coming to tickle you."

She laughed, darted left, he went right, tripped over Cap, and ended up sprawled on the ground, with Cap dancing around like this was the best game ever.

"Cap! Run! Don't let the Bommibal snowman get ya!"

I joined in, and it was one of those perfect crystal moments I would remember for the rest of my life.

When we all calmed down, following a rendition of

Jason-the-Bommibal-snowman playing drums using the back of the sofa, and Daisy rolling on the floor with laughter as Cap barked along with Jason, it was time for the grand light switch-on.

I held one of Daisy's hands, Jason held the other, and then after a countdown that had Cap prancing about in front of the tree like crazy, I switched on the lights, and the front room was filled with a hundred tiny twinkling lights flashing in random colors. Then it was time for hot chocolate, the pizza we'd ordered in, and sitting on the sofa in front of our tree.

Daisy didn't last long, yawning widely, and Jason carried her up to bed. I saw to Cap, locked up, and then went upstairs, catching the tail end of a story as Daisy was drifting to sleep. Jason turned off the lights, made sure Daisy was tucked in, and then saw me at the door. The flare of hope and affection might only have been quick, but I saw it.

I held out a hand, which he took, and then I tugged him to my bedroom.

We were in no hurry as we stripped in the darkness, kissing each other on every spare inch of skin revealed by touch alone until we were both naked, and hard against each other.

"Fuck me," Jason said, shoving me a little toward the bed.

"Slow down," I encouraged, but I quickly found myself on my back, my cast catching on the covers, and everything wrong and messy. I yanked him down with me, but as he hit the bed, I used the momentum and pinned him under me. "Slow. Down."

"We don't have all the time in the fucking world,"

Jason growled, and I desperately wanted to say that yes, we did, but then I'd be lying when I knew he was waiting to run even now.

"I'm not rushing this," I said, and nipped at his collar bone, and then lower, drawing one nipple into my mouth and sucking until he whimpered under his breath, and then biting gently and so fast I thought he'd miss it, only he didn't, and he groaned and arched up under me.

"More," he demanded, but I wasn't going to give in like that, this was happening on my timescale, and I worried at the other nipple in the same way. "Jesus, move will you," he muttered, and I reached over and turned on the bedside light then I covered his mouth with my hand so he couldn't talk.

"Do I have to gag you?" I asked, and his eyes widened. "Would you like that, huh? I might have a cast, but I can pin you down. Then you couldn't talk at all, and if I tied you down you wouldn't be able to run, and I could spend all night taking you to the edge, one finger inside you, my mouth on your cock, and then I could leave you there, tied to my bed, and I'd get off on you, but I wouldn't let you come…" I moved my hand. "Shhh," I ordered and waited until he nodded. Then I carried on, kissing my way down his body, stopping at each slope and dip of his muscles, making sure to mark the sensitive skin that I could. I kissed the faint burn marks on his side and then spent a long time pressing butterfly kisses to the corded scar on his arm, my hand on his cock, twisting it and holding it, too gentle for him to come. I kept it up for so long that a few more strokes and I swear he'd be coming.

"In me," he pleaded.

I smiled into a kiss, reaching for the things we needed. "Uh-huh?" I warned him.

"Please, Leo, fuck, please."

I loved that he was pleading, and not demanding, that somehow in all of this, he was giving up control and losing himself to sensation and not dwelling on the pain and worries in his life. I rolled onto my back, smoothing a condom on my cock, and watched him as he loosened himself with lube. I played with his cock, getting him to the point where he was thrusting down into my grip and then forcing himself back on my finger, and only then, after I was sure he was ready, I held myself steady and he edged down. I paused, then pushed, then paused, and it seemed to take forever to get where I wanted to be, but he was rocking on me, and pleading and I helped him move so his hips and ass were supported and he helped me to stay steady with my cast.

Then we made the slowest, deepest love and all I could think was that this man had stolen his way into my life and made me dream of the future.

He rode me slowly, the pleading had died down to nothing but thready breathing, and he wouldn't let me move.

"So close," I murmured, and circled his cock again. When he came, he bent over double and hid his face in my neck, and when I lost it, I turned my face into his hair.

And somewhere between coming into this room, and sex, I'd fallen in love.

I just needed to make him see it too, and to explain some of the things I'd done and seen. He could listen, then he could run, or he could at least attempt to stay. With my heart beating frantically in my chest I took a quick breath and then forged ahead.

"I was adopted you know," I murmured, as Jason snuggled into my neck. I loved having him there, curled up with me, and I wanted more of this.

"Yeah, I know."

"My mom died a few months before my fifth birthday. And my dad..." This wasn't as easy as I hoped it would be, but Jason took my hand and held on tight, as if he knew how hard this was for me. "... let's just say he was my biological dad, and he came from nowhere when my mom passed away." I paused then, because the next part of this shitty life story would scare anyone away. After all, who would want to take on damaged goods?

"How did your mom die?" He asked the question softly, and I nearly didn't catch all of it, but it was the obvious place to start.

"Overdose, she was twenty-three. We lived in this community right next to a river, and it was full of alternative lifestyle moms and dads. One day she didn't wake up, that's all." I stopped again, because he didn't need to know the rest, but he kissed my neck to reassure me, and suddenly it was all too easy to talk. "I found her."

He made a soft noise of distress, and squeezed my hand again. "I'm so sorry."

"Nothing for you to be sorry about, it's out there, you know? But, I do remember her not waking up, and I recall the day when *he* turned up. His name was Jeff, and he was a giant of a man, or at least he was to me. I was little and he was an adult, and he was strong."

He raised his head and I glanced at him briefly. There

was understanding in his gaze, and emotion crawled out from inside the darkest places where I hid it.

"You don't have to tell me any more," he whispered. "It's okay."

"No, it's not okay. You have to understand that there's a reason I shoved you against a wall when I thought you'd hurt Daisy, and there's a reason why I don't talk about what it was like back then. It has to come out and be there for you to see, so then you can trust I would never let anyone hurt Daisy."

"I do trust you," he said, but I cupped the back of his head and held him still. I had to make him *see* the real me.

"I was with him for a year, and he hurt me, mentally and physically. I was just a little kid, and he made my life hell."

"Fuck," Jason groaned, and kissed my cheek, pressing his face there and holding me close. "What happened to him?"

"He died in a bar fight."

"Good," he said, fiercely.

"The system, and then Mama and Papa Byrne saved me from more like him. I was one of the lucky ones. I will always carry the memories, because I can't forget. I've seen experts, and I have a family that loves me, and friends that mean everything to me, but the acid is still inside me."

He let go of my hand and propped himself up on his elbows, kissed me very gently.

"Then you're the bravest man I know," he murmured. "To fight and carry on."

TWENTY-TWO

Jason

———————

WHAT LEO TOLD me meant that it took some time to fall asleep, the thoughts of what had happened to Leo when he was a child burned inside me, and it was only when his breathing evened out that I slept.

An insistent buzzing woke me, and I recognized my burner phone, but I ignored it for two reasons. One, I couldn't reach it given I was buried in a pile of blanket and half covered by a heavy breathing Leo, and two, I didn't really want to move from under Leo anyway.

Leo.

I had to admit the obvious. For him, it wasn't sex. After what he'd told me last night it was obvious that for him, it was hope and promise and forever. I wish I had the luxury of those kinds of feelings, but I had Daisy to think about, and Rain.

"Whassup?" Leo mumbled, and I buried my fingers in his hair. If this was it, if this was all I could have, then I wanted to remember everything about him, from the texture of his hair to his stupid-ass broken leg, to the way he made hot chocolate.

"Nothing," I murmured and glanced at the clock, which showed it was only a little after five. What was it with Austin and his ridiculous texts at ass o'clock in the morning? I wriggled my hand free from where it had been trapped and reached for the cell, fumbling with it as it fell on the bed, and cursing under my breath as I fished it out of the folds of material. I messed around a little more trying to get the damn thing to unlock, and finally, there it was, a text from Austin.

Rain is awake. Call me.

Calmly, carefully, I shut the phone and closed my eyes.

"What's wrong?" Leo asked, and slid from over me, sitting back on his arms and glancing at me with a cautious expression.

"Rain is awake," I said all matter-of-fact, even though my stomach was churning, and my heart hurt. This was good news, Daisy's mom was awake, so why did the update come with a side helping of sick dread?

I couldn't look at Leo all patient and compassionate and wanting me to stay. Because what we had was nothing, and it was over.

"I'm checking on Daisy and getting a shower," I announced, and slipped out of bed, yanking on my shorts and T, and opening Leo's door.

"Jason, wait," he called, but I shook my head.

"Not now," I said, and shut the door behind me.

I spent a few moments just staring down at Daisy, who was sleeping in a ball, her stuffed dragon in her arms, then I tucked loose covers back around her and went to the shower. In short order, I was showered, dressed, and heading for coffee, not surprised to see that Leo had beaten me to it, and handed me a coffee as soon as I entered the kitchen. There was so much unspoken between us, fear and anger, and resignation, but I couldn't give a voice to those words, so I stayed silent as we sat out on the patio and watched the sky lighten. It was Cap who told us someone was at the door, with the whole tugging at Leo's arm, but when I heard Cap barking, I went inside to see what was wrong, only to find Leo and Austin clearly doing the introduction thing, and shaking hands with respect.

I snapped out of my worried misery. "What are you doing here?"

Austin extended his hand, but I ignored it. "I texted you about Rain," he said instead.

"I know you did."

"And I asked you to call me," he sounded so patient, and for some reason, I wanted to punch him in his perfect square-jawed stubbled face.

"Fuck you, Austin. I needed time," to wake up, come to terms, think, strategize.

He held up his hands. "We have a sensitive issue and a chance to resolve this once and for all."

"Resolve what, exactly?" Leo asked and crossed his arms over his chest. Right now, I wanted him to deal with the Fed, to take away the confusion that knotted inside me.

"Billy is in the area, he was spotted at the hospital, but he got away from us."

I exploded, "He's a fucking drug addict with no brains. How the hell did you let him get away?"

Austin tilted his chin. "He's clearly had experience evading the cops," he said, although it sounded too much like an excuse for my liking. "We just need you and Daisy to visit Rain and—"

"No," Leo snapped.

A muscle twitched at Austin's temple. "Look, it's the one way where we can be sure that—"

"No," Leo repeated facing off Austin, whose expression had turned hard and determined.

I stepped between them. "What the hell?"

"You tell him," Leo said, "tell him you want him and Daisy as bait in the hospital to draw out Billy."

Austin frowned. "I don't need to, because you just did."

They began to shout around me, and I had to raise my voice to be heard. "I'll do it," I thundered.

Leo grabbed me and pulled me away from Austin. "But—"

"Just me. Daisy will stay with Leo," I was talking to Austin but staring right at Leo.

"It's Daisy he's been looking for—"

"No," it was my turn to draw the line. "I'll visit Rain, and we'll make it obvious, and if he's in the vicinity, then I'll draw him out, but I won't put Daisy in a position where she gets hurt."

"Jason, please, you need to think this through," Leo demanded, but I was done with hiding.

I stiffened my spine and turned to Austin. "Let's do this."

"He'll meet you at the car," Leo stopped me from leaving, his grip hard on my arm. I let him hold me because I needed the breathing time, and after a moment's pause, Austin gave a sharp nod and went out the front door.

"What are you doing?" Leo asked, and I didn't have an answer for him that would make sense.

"Promise me that you'll look after Daisy, don't let her leave your sight."

"Of course—"

"Nothing will happen to me."

"You don't know that, I've seen these things go south before."

"I won't let it," I was defiant.

"How?"

He seemed like he was lost for words, and he wasn't the only one, then he gripped my arms. "I love you," he announced with great authority, "and I know you love me back."

I shrugged free, and luckily I didn't have to lie to him, because Daisy walked into the kitchen, trailing her dragon, her eyes bleary, "Was you shouting, Daddy?"

I scooped her up and held her close. I didn't need to tell her I loved her, or that I would be back, she didn't have to know I was even going to see her mom. "I need to go out for a while. I'll be back soon."

"M'kay," she yawned and cuddled into me, still warm from the bed.

"I think Cap needs his kibble," I said and handed her to Leo, who was in shock. "Everything will be okay."

And then I left, and the lie that I was going to tell was bitter in my mouth.

Because I was going to tell him the biggest lie of all—I was going to say I could never love him.

When I'd actually fallen headlong into love a long time ago.

THE HOSPITAL WAS busy even though it was six a.m. The plan was simple, we'd arrive outside, make a show of me visiting, and I'd head inside, be taken to Rain's room. Then everyone would wait and see what happened. As plans went, it was pretty shit, but if I spotted Billy, it wouldn't be me getting beaten up and choked. He wouldn't get the jump on me this time. Fired with the need to protect myself and my family, I headed inside. A nurse showed me to the room, eyes darting left and right, which made me think she wasn't a nurse at all, and finally, we were in room three-twenty-five.

"We have eyes on you," the nurse whisperer, so yeah, definitely not a real nurse.

It was a big hospital, and it had taken an hour to get there, and the more distance there was between Leo and me, the less I was able to convince myself that if anything did go wrong, then he could help me.

I was in this alone, and when I stepped into the room with a single bed, and the machines, I felt even more alone. Rain looked so tired, thin, helpless, and nothing like the firebrand she'd been when I'd first met her. Any vitality she'd had had been drained by the drugs and the overdose and with Billy's help. At least she wasn't on a ventilator, but when she spoke, her voice was scratchy as though maybe they'd not long removed the tube.

"Jason?" she half-whispered. "Is Daisy here?"

"I left her at home for now," I explained and approached the bed, taking her hand in mine.

"Will you tell her it wasn't me, that I didn't do it."

"Do what?" I needed her to be more specific, but she

coughed, and I gave her water until the chest spasms had stopped.

"I wouldn't leave Daisy, I tried not to leave her, but he was… I wasn't strong enough, not even for her."

This didn't sound as if she was demanding I bring Daisy, that she was going to get up out of bed and take our daughter somewhere I wouldn't find her. She was choking, quiet, sad.

"Okay," I encouraged. However deep her addiction was, I at least understood some of the pieces of the puzzle that led her here—overbearing father, rebellion, drugs, pregnancy, running from her dad, falling in with Billy.

The door opened behind us, and I tensed because the last thing I wanted was the Feds hovering around me with Rain doing so poorly. She was trying to talk, and I wanted to listen to her because I felt protective, and she was vulnerable and… most of all, because of Daisy. I turned to see who had come into the room. Billy, with one hand gripping the hair of the nurse who'd shown me in, and in the other hand, a deadly looking gun right against her temple. He was backing into the room, using her as a shield, and in front of him were two agents, one of them Austin, both with their sidearms out.

"Tell them to back down," Billy snapped at me, and I caught Austin's gaze. He was icily focused, but the nurse was in the way, between a bullet and Billy. No one was dying here, and I couldn't help but think there was a certain inevitability to this moment.

"I've got this," I said with as much conviction as I could manage.

Austin shook his head, but all I could think was that I

could talk Billy down. He didn't want to kill me, or Rain, he just wanted money.

"I said, I've got this," I snapped, and Austin showed only the smallest sign that he'd heard me. They backed off a little, just outside the room, and Billy, in a quick move, came to me, shoved the nurse away and instead, pointed the gun at my temple. I saw Austin move to take a shot, but Billy wasn't stupid, in fact he seemed icily focused right now, and it was my turn to be a human shield. There was too much of a chance of collateral damage here and Austin knew it.

"Get the fuck out of here," Billy growled at the nurse, who crab-walked to the door, where Austin helped her up. "Shut the fucking door."

I nodded to Austin. "It'll be okay."

For the longest time Billy was silent, alternating between gripping my hair, and yanking me back, "Jason," he finally said, and for a moment I wondered if he would drop the gun, but he didn't, it was fixed and firm, and he curled a hand even harder in my hair to hold my head still. A hundred things flew through my mind, twisting and turning, then blending into one thing—Daisy. I wasn't going to die here.

"Billy," I answered just as evenly and attempted to remain calm. "You know the cops will be out there when you try to leave."

"Yep, FBI as well. I'm fucking big," he sounded so damn proud, and something clicked inside me, out of all my random thoughts, I could see one scenario where this ended with Billy committing suicide by cop. How could he even think he would escape this?

"You can still stop."

He yanked me back and away from Rain, shoving me to the floor, the gun wavering a little but still ending up on me. "I just wanted money," he mumbled, "I owe money all over, and I ain't a coward, but I'm fucked, and all I wanted was the kid, so I got money, and *she* got in the way." He waved the gun at Rain, and I tensed. If I pushed up hard enough, I could get between him and Rain, maybe stop him from carrying his abuse to the end.

"Talk to me," I said.

"You wanna know something? She wouldn't tell me where she'd put Daisy, told me you had her, then she laughed at me. But she fought like a tiger." He pulled down his collar, showing me three deep welts, scars from cuts or something else, nails maybe? "And even when I forced those pills down her throat, told her I wanted the kid, she refused. An' then, when I found you... the kid wasn't even there... it's all fucked. All fucked." He shook his head.

Was he slurring his words? He was rambling, as if he was giving some huge bad guy speech—grandstanding and dramatic.

"I can get you money," I lied.

"You?" he spat on the floor. "You can't get no fucking money, and hers is all gone, and the cops are all over the hospital. You think I didn't see 'em. Fuck, I had to shove one down a stairwell to even get here, arrogant fucker didn't even think I could take her, dressed as a fucking nurse, do they think I'm stupid..." He coughed, retched, and patted his chest. The gun shook again, and his words slipped and slid out in confusion and chaos. He pulled something else out of his light jacket, a long thin stiletto of a knife, and he balanced it on his fingers, but it wobbled and wouldn't stay right, which seemed to confuse him. Cautiously, I moved a little, pulling myself up on the bed, but even with the gun, he wasn't a danger to anyone but himself. He was a pathetic mess, and the knife dropped to the floor.

"We can get you help," I sidled between him and Rain, focusing on protecting Daisy's mom because that at least gave me a purpose.

"No one can help me now. All I wanted was fucking money. Her dad has it all…" he coughed again, and blood flecked his lips.

"Billy—"

"So fucked," he interrupted and stepped back, with only the wall holding him up. Then for the longest time, he stood there, the gun pointed at me, and his breathing grew shallow.

Were the agents working out a way to get inside? Did they think that we were both dead? *They would have heard if he'd killed us with a gun, but he had a knife.*

"This stuff is good," he muttered, "everything is like cotton candy."

He grinned then, and looked vacantly at the gun, waving it in front of him.

"What stuff?" I asked, and hoped to hell he didn't accidentally fire the pistol.

"Good stuff, so they'll never get me," he said.

Before I could reply, there was a noise, a pop, shattering glass.

I didn't know what it was, but the gun fell from Billy's hands and the tiniest amount of blood trickled from a neat hole in his forehead. He was dead before he hit the floor, a trail of scarlet, the worst evidence of his death behind him, smeared down the wall.

And behind me, Rain began to scream.

———————

"He took out a fucking agent!" I heard Leo shout for the fifth time, but it seemed no one was listening to him. Rain and I held hands and stayed calm as chaos spun around us; a nurse checked Rain, not the same pretend nurse who'd been used as a human shield and who was being treated for shock, but another one called Zoe, who patted my arm a lot. First, they'd removed Billy's body, then told us he'd been taken out by a single bullet from a sniper bullet on the roof opposite. Turned out we'd made the news, and the ten or so minutes I thought we'd been inside the room with Billy as he slowly lost his grip on life, had actually been more like forty. The room swarmed with people, all armed, and finally, far too fast for him to have come from home, Leo entered the room, took one look at me, the blood on the wall, and stalked out again before loudly losing his shit with anyone who would listen. Sean was there with him, and it was Sean who came over to me and side-hugged me.

"Daisy is with Asher, I drove Leo here," he explained in quick sentences, probably used to summing up a situation in as few words as possible.

"I want to see Daisy," Rain said and then coughed again until I gave her water. "She will want to see her mom."

"Okay," I said, even as my heart broke. Rain had tried to save Daisy, she hadn't *deliberately* overdosed, but she'd been using, and even if I could accept that shit, how could I even imagine a life where Daisy wasn't with *me*?

"I want to take her somewhere safe," Rain shouted, and yanked at the cannula. Sean stopped her, held her hand, and shushed her.

"I won't let you take her," I said with determination.

"She's my daughter, I want her safe."

The words spilled out of me before I even knew what I was saying. "Daisy is my daughter, as well. Wherever you go, I go, and we'll share her care, or I'll fight you for her."

Rain sobbed loudly, and then abruptly she stopped, as if the clouds had cleared from her thoughts. "You won't have to, I can't... we can... talk..."

"Later, sleep now," Sean encouraged.

She closed her eyes, and I was impressed by his Super-Doctor powers.

Leo grabbed me as soon as I stepped outside the room, tugged me away from Rain and Sean and over to a fire exit door, shoving it open and pulling me through. He was instantly right up in my face, not caring who might follow us.

"I said I love you," he snapped, his words forceful, demanding a response, "and you never answered me."

This time it was my turn to gentle him, cradling his face and kissing him.

"I love you," I said because that was all there was to say. The buts, and the maybes, and the indefinite future was something for another time. Right now, I needed Daisy, and I sure as hell needed to be in love with this man.

Because they were my everything.

Epilogue

JASON - 1 YEAR and a few days later

"… happy birthday dear Day-zeeeeeeeee, happy birthday to you."

Everyone sang to the birthday girl, who had a brand new Disney dress, with an added tiara from her Uncle Ash. Mama Byrne had pulled this entire party from nothing after the hall we'd booked had flooded, and we were at our house, in the tidy garden, with Christmas and party decorations hanging from every tree and bush. The happy birthdays segued into Christmas carols, and I stepped back from the madness of the party to find a quiet space so I could think about my life and how wonderful it was right now. I could go into my brand new drumming room, an insulated shed in the garden that Leo, Sean, and Eric had built. It had AC, a coffee machine, and held a shiny drum kit—my present from Leo, on my last birthday.

I went in there when things became too much, losing myself in the percussion and passion that I loved. I'd even made inroads into playing with a band again, just a local group who played in school halls, but yeah, the fire was back in my blood. Leo said there was nothing sexier than a drummer's biceps, which meant it was a win/win situation for us both. We'd worked hard to make a stable life for ourselves, and the hopes we had for the future were bright. Daisy's primary residency was with me and Leo, oh, and Cap, who loved the new turn of events. That he slept in her room every night was just a sign of his devotion. Either that or he really liked pink, which was the predominant color in there along with the vast hedgehog hotel. Also what seemed like two hundred resident prickly little assholes that were hell to walk on in the dead of night.

Asher and Sean's adoption had been finalized and their newest daughter, Melanie, stayed over sometimes, she too seemed to like pink, and hedgehogs, and at around the same age as Daisy, they'd become close.

Rain had completed a long spell in rehab, and she was on a long road to recovery, but she was working hard on making herself present in Daisy's life again, and we were working just as hard on being friends after all of this. Her dad was behind bars, and never asked to see her or Daisy, but that was no significant loss, and one day he would realize what he'd lost, only it would be too late to see what an amazing little girl Daisy was. Billy wasn't even mentioned in any conversation now, and counseling had helped her as much as Daisy. In fact, Rain had met a painter called Dan who worked for Jax, and they were engaged coming on a month now. One day, I guess I would have to share Daisy's time more than I did now, but for Daisy, I would do anything.

Talking of Jax, he *was* supposed to be there, but yet again, he'd vanished to another city in the hope of finding

Zachary, although this trip to Calgary was full of optimism. Who knows, but he'd been spending a lot of time hunched over paperwork in our kitchen with his brother, so maybe there was hope.

As for Leo and me? Well, after that day in the hospital with Billy, I'd finally accepted that Leo and I had a future together. He was the one who'd encouraged me to go to college, and after ignoring him for the longest time and holding down a crappy job in a warehouse, I'd given in. I'd thought about chiropractic care, astronomy, and history, but ended up choosing Math and Computing, which was far from easy on my sometimes exhausted brain, but it seemed I had transferrable skills from my hacking days and a flair with numbers. Still, I was a semester in, and things were good. I had financial support from the college, a part-time job at the café in the park near our house, walked Daisy to a local preschool, and picked her up when I could, and balancing childcare between us, everything was perfect.

In fact, life had become the very thing I'd thought I couldn't have.

Lillian visited with Daisy every so often, but Daisy remembered little about Billy, or about me being hurt, choosing to remember other more important days. Like the one when Cap had jumped over the back fence, or the day he'd eaten one of my shoes. But, what was even more impressive was that Leo was talking to Lillian as well, informally, as he peeled back the layers of the childhood he'd had before he was adopted. Somehow, with Lillian's help he confronted old ghosts, and we talked for ages about what he was remembered.

That is what we did best as a family; we talked about

everything *except* for some of what he saw at work.

Still, he, Eric, and Sean still met up every week, when they could, to sit in silence at the bottom of the yard. But when they were done, and they'd relaxed and chilled with Cap, the evening ended with me and Leo sharing hot chocolate in our yard and then time alone.

Sometimes he told me about his day, and sometimes he didn't.

Either way, it didn't change the way I felt about him or the hope I had for the future.

"Cake?" Leo handed me a paper plate with a slice of the lemon cake I'd baked. That was another thing I was doing in my spare time, and I felt domesticated when I was wearing an apron and covered in flour. Leo, on the other hand, said I looked so sexy he couldn't keep his hands off me. It worked either way.

"I can't believe Daisy's five today," I said, and then forked some cake with a huge dollop of buttercream frosting into my mouth.

Leo was way ahead of me, his slice was nearly gone, and he was making these noises that bordered on pornographic as he scooped up the last bit.

"Me neither," he said and wiped his mouth on a paper napkin.

"School soon," I added.

"Yep."

"And it's Christmas in two days, and we haven't wrapped all her presents yet." I gestured at the lights hung in the trees, and the glow of them on the huge Christmas tree in our living room. Daisy had made decorations with Leo and we had the tree up at Thanksgiving much to Mama Byrne's delight. It had been while they were busy decorating the tree that she'd first called him Papa. He'd never asked her to, but she matter-of-factly told him that he was her papa, and that was the end of it all. He didn't argue, but he did get emotional, and I think we both shed a few tears when we were alone in our room later that night.

"We'll get to wrapping it all," he said, "I'm off tomorrow and I bought the extra wrapping paper."

"Why do we need more paper? I thought we'd decided we're not wrapping each new hedgehog individually." He gave me that look where I knew that was exactly what we'd be doing.

I ate some more cake, watched Daisy and Melanie run around with Cap, shouting and laughing as they did.

"Jason?"

"Hmm?" I turned to face Leo, but he wasn't where I expected him to be. It took me a moment to realize he was kneeling on the ground next to me and another moment to comprehend that he was holding out a small velvet box, opened, and showing two perfect rings.

"Will you marry me?" he asked, very simply—nothing fancy, just careful words and with love in his eyes.

"That's an easy answer," I said, and crouched down next to him, placing my cake plate on the grass.

"Is it?" he said, and I touched his cheek.

And in the garden in front of our family and friends, with Cap depositing a Frisbee at our feet and eating the rest of my cake because no one was stopping him, I said the only word that made any sense at all.

"Yes."

THE END

What's next in single Dads?

Single | Today | Promise | *Always* | *Listen*

Always, book 4 (April 2020)

Firefighter Adam's life changed in an instant. Cameron is haunted by his past. Can one small boy show these two men that bravery starts in their hearts

Saving a child trapped in a car wasn't firefighter Adam being a hero; it was instinct. When the injuries he suffers means he can no longer do the job he loved, he turns to a new way of making a difference, working with children who have lost family in fire.

When his family is torn apart by tragedy, Cameron isn't able to make any sense of his life. Working in construction on a children's home is part of his healing process, but sometimes the days never end, and he knows he's losing his way. How can he be a father to his son, when all he wants to do is mourn?

Single Dads, book 4, coming to an e-reader near you in April 2020

Sign up for a release reminder at rjscott.co.uk

What's next for RJ Scott

_____

Lancaster Falls

Mystery / Murder / Suspense Romance

What Lies Beneath | Without a Trace | All That Remains

Without A Trace (book 2) - 21 February 2020

When long-buried secrets are exposed, and the search for truth becomes a race to save a life, how can two men ever hope to find real love?

Losing his brother has shaped Drew to become the man he is today—heartbroken, alone, but determined to make a difference in the world. Joining the military, fighting battles in places that he's never even heard of, is his attempt to make amends for telling his brother to go to hell. After his brother disappeared, he'd clung to the hope Casey was out there living his life. Of course, he'd be furious at Drew, and probably hate his brother, but at least in Drew's head, Casey was safe.

One call changes everything. Casey's body has been found, and the hope that had fueled Drew's constant search for the truth is destroyed. Coming home to Lancaster Falls to bury his brother and face his mom's anguish and accusations, is a nightmare made real, and he has nowhere to run from the pain.

Logan has made a home in Lancaster Falls. As a police officer, he plays by the rules, and he would never think of working off-the-grid. All that changes when an anonymous tip crosses his desk, and he is thrust headlong into solving a hundred-year mystery that could be connected with the modern day death of Casey McGuire. Fighting an attraction to Casey's brother is hard enough, but the infuriating man is there at Logan's every turn, interfering with the case, breaking the rules, and demanding that Casey's story be heard.

Newsletter

To keep up to date with news and releases then I have a monthly newsletter alongside tailored bulletins for different sales outlets whenever there is a new release, or I make a book free, or have a sale.

You can select which newsletter groups you want to sign up for and it all starts here:

Sign up for a release reminder at rjscott.co.uk

Also by RJ Scott

Single Dads

Single | Today | Promise | Always (Apr 2020) | Listen (July 2020)

Lancaster Falls

What Lies Beneath | Without a Trace (Jan 2020) | All that Remains (Mar 2020)

Texas

The Heart of Texas | Texas Winter | Texas Heat | Texas Family | Texas Christmas | Texas Fall | Texas Wedding | Texas Gift | Home For Christmas

Legacy (spin-off from Texas series)

Kyle | Gabriel | Daniel

Montana

Crooked Tree Ranch | The Rancher's Son | A Cowboy's Home | Snow In Montana | Second Chance Ranch | Montana Sky

Wyoming

Winter Cowboy | Summer Drifter

Action Adventure Romance

Heroes, Bodyguards, First Responders, SEALs, Marines, Cops

Sanctuary

Guarding Morgan | The Only Easy Day | Face Value | Still Waters | Full Circle | The Journal of Sanctuary 1 | World's Collide | Accidental Hero | Ghost | By The Numbers

A Reason To Stay | Last Marine Standing | Deacon's Law

Bodyguards Inc

Bodyguard to a Sex God | The Ex-Factor | Max and the Prince | Undercover Lovers | Love's Design | Kissing Alex

Standalone

Alpha Delta | Seth & Casey

All The King's Men | Retrograde | Force of Nature

Hockey Romance

Standalone Titles

Secrets | Dallas Christmas | Last Chance

Hockey Romance written with V.L. Locey

Harrisburg Railers

Changing Lines | First Season | Deep Edge | Poke Check| Last Defense | Goal Line | Neutral Zone | Hat Trick | Save the Date

Owatonna U

Ryker | Scott | Benoit

Arizona Raptors

Coast To Coast

Small Town / First Responders Romance

Ellery Mountain

The Fireman and the Cop | The Teacher and the Soldier | The Carpenter and the Actor | The Doctor and the Bad Boy | The Paramedic and the Writer | The Barman and the SEAL | The Agent and the Model | The Sinner and the Saint

Christmas Romance

The Christmas Throwaway | Love Happens Anyway | New York Christmas | The Christmas Collection | Jesse's Christmas | The Road to Frosty Hollow | Christmas Prince | Dallas Christmas | Angel in a Book Shop | Mr Sparkles

Standalone Romance Stories

One Night | Moments | Back Home | Boy Banned | Deefur Dog | Child Of The Storm | Spirit Bear | The Decisions We Make (YA/NA) | The Bucket List | The Summer House | Three (MMM) | How Much For The Whole Night | For a Rainy Afternoon | Snow & Secrets

Written with Meredith Russell

Sapphire Cay

Follow the Sun | Under the Sun | Chase The Sun | Christmas In The Sun | Capture The Sun | Forever In The Sun

Boyfriends For Hire

Darcy | Kaden

Standalone

The Art of Words | The Road to Frosty Hollow

Written with Chris Quinton

Salisbury

Heat | Ice

Paranormal Romance

Standalone Stories

The Gallows Tree | The New Wolf | The Soldier's Tale | Ghost In
The Stone (Coming Halloween 2019)

In the Shadow of the Wolf

With Diane Adams

Shattered Secrets | Broken Memories | Splintered Lies

Oracle

Oracle | Book of Secrets | The Oracle Collection

End Street Detective Agency

With Amber Kell

End Street Volume 1 (Cupid Curse / Wicked Wolf) | End Street

Meet RJ Scott

RJ is the author of the over one hundred published novels and discovered romance in books at a very young age. She realized that if there wasn't romance on the page, she could create it in her head, and is a lifelong writer. She lives and works out of her home in the beautiful English countryside, spends her spare time reading, watching films, and enjoying time with her family. The last time she had a week's break from writing she didn't like it one little bit and has yet to meet a bottle of wine she couldn't defeat.

www.rjscott.co.uk | rj@rjscott.co.uk

I'm an APP!
Go to app.rjscott.co.uk on your phone
and never miss another release!

facebook.com/author.rjscott

twitter.com/Rjscott_author

instagram.com/rjscott_author

bookbub.com/authors/rj-scott

pinterest.com/rjscottauthor